W9-DHW-434

Storm at Daybreak

DAYBREAK MYSTERY

B·J·HOFF

ACCENT BOOKS
CHARIOT FAMILY PUBLISHING
A DIVISION OF DAVID C. COOK PUBLISHING CO.

Accent Books™ is an imprint of David C. Cook Publishing Co.
David C. Cook Publishing Co., Elgin, Illinois 60120
David C. Cook Publishing Co., Weston, Ontario
Nova Distribution Ltd., Newton Abbot, England

STORM AT DAYBREAK
©1986 by B.J. Hoff

Cover design by Koechel/Peterson & Associates, Inc.

First Printing, 1986
Printed in the United States of America
96 95 94 93 92 7 6 5 4 3

Library of Congress Catalog Card Number 86-70645
ISBN 0-78140-519-X

*This book is dedicated
to Anne ... who planted—
to Jo Ann ... who pruned—
and to Cheryl ... who prayed ...*

Forever faithful ... Forever friends ...

AUTHOR'S NOTE:

The town of Shepherd Valley, West Virginia, is fictional. The majestic beauty of the mountains and the indomitable spirit of the people are wonderfully real.

My sincere thanks to the Governor's Office of Economic & Community Development and the Chamber of Commerce of West Virginia for their generous assistance.

Thanks, also, to Ms. Catherine W. Swan, The Seeing Eye, Inc., Morristown, New Jersey.

He heals the bird with the broken wing...
He heals the child with a broken dream...
He heals the one with a broken heart...
Our Lord makes all broken things whole.

B.J. Hoff
From "Broken Wings"

Prologue

The narrow road was slick and treacherous. Patches of ice checkered the pavement. Most of them were barely noticeable beneath a light, frosty layer of drifting snow. The thin, nervous man behind the steering wheel of a battered red pickup swerved, narrowly avoiding a ditch, when the voice came over the radio. With an edgy glance in the rearview mirror, he pulled off the highway, bumping and skidding over a rough, frozen mound of snow. When the truck finally pitched to a stop, he let the engine idle as he turned up the volume on the radio.

The heater was working for a change, but he turned the fan on low so he could hear better. He hated the voice, but he had to listen. It was important that he listen every day now.

His mouth quivered, and he wiped a bony, talon-fingered hand across it impatiently. Kaine was at it again with his holier-than-thou hogwash. *He had his nerve, didn't he? Who gave him the right to get on that microphone of his and tell the whole town—the whole county—what to do?* A dull, thick ache began to wreathe his head and heat his anger even more. He pushed a stained hunting cap further back on his head, then tucked a limp strand of faded brown hair underneath it.

Thinks he's real funny this morning. The man especially hated Saturdays because Kaine talked more then. Other days he mostly played that church music of his and didn't say much. But on Saturdays he talked a lot.

Now he was talking about that big radiothon of his. The man ran the back of one hand slowly down his leg, snagging a split fingernail on the torn seam of his jeans. His mouth was dry, and he tried to swallow but couldn't. He licked his lips, then twisted them in a sneer at his own sour taste.

The voice on the radio made a few more brief comments about a nationwide campaign to increase the drunk driving penalties. The man snorted, a broken, phlegmy sound in the muffled quiet of the truck. *Something ought to be done about that big, mouthy ape. Got the whole town thinkin' he's so special, so important. Just because he owns a radio station. A Christian radio station. Just because he's different, not a normal man. Maybe everybody wouldn't think he was such a prize if they knew. If they knew about my kid.*

He squinted through the icy glaze forming on the windshield, his eyes watering as he listened. *Somebody needs to shut him up. He talks too much. He's got nothing else to do, that's his problem. So he spends his time preachin' over the radio.*

No wife or kids, of course. The man laughed aloud, a sharp, ugly sound. *No woman'd have the likes of Kaine, that was a fact. A woman wants a normal man. He'll never have himself any kids of his own, so he tries to take someone else's boy.*

He framed his narrow, weathered face between calloused hands, pressing his fingertips to his temples. *I'm sick of you, Kaine . . . sick of thinking about you, sick of the sound of you. One of these days, somebody's gonna pull the plug on you, shut you up for good.*

1

Jennifer glanced around the radio station's lobby, hoping to see a receptionist. When she didn't, she walked straight ahead toward two glass-enclosed studios. A tall, lanky teenage boy with mournful eyes was vacuuming the empty studio on the left. He exchanged a shy grin with Jennifer through the glass partition, then returned to his work.

Catching a glimpse of her reflection in an oak-framed wall mirror, Jennifer stopped for a moment to make a quick inspection of herself. Three hours plus behind the wheel of her aging Honda had left her feeling rumpled, stiff, and at a definite disadvantage for her interview with Daniel Kaine. She searched the cluttered depths of her shoulder bag for a comb. Finding none, she made a futile attempt to smooth her heavy chestnut hair with her fingers, then tried in vain to brush away some of the wrinkles in her gold corduroy suit. After a moment, she lifted one cynical eyebrow in defeat and shrugged philosophically.

Sensing movement out of the corner of her eye, she turned to the studio on her right. A lone disc jockey was sprawled comfortably in a worn brown chair, adjusting his headset as he spoke into a suspension microphone.

The two years she'd spent in Rome studying voice with Carlo Paulo had conditioned her to a steady parade of intriguing, attractive men. While not exactly immune to their appeal, she considered herself difficult to impress. At the moment, however, Jennifer was definitely impressed.

He wasn't handsome. At least not in the conventional sense. He had the look of a vagabond prince, she thought fancifully. A touch of nobility subtly blended with a touch of the maverick. He was a big man, obviously. His shoulders seemed to go on forever, and, even slouched as he was with one leg thrown idly over the arm of his chair, she could see that he would tower several inches over her. At five-eight she didn't run into that too often.

She moved closer, nearly touching her nose to the glass window. As she watched, the disc jockey leaned casually back in his chair, placing one large hand on the control board and the other on his headset to make an adjustment. His red V-neck sweater emphasized deeply tanned skin that looked to be naturally dark without any help from the sun. His long legs were sheathed in jeans so worn they were practically a disgrace. His hair was an odd shade of charcoal—not quite, but almost black, a peculiar dusky color. A startling line of silver winged randomly along the left side, from his temple upward, fading into the thick, dark strands that fell over his forehead.

Fascinated, Jennifer dryly reminded herself that she didn't care for beards, although his was thick and neatly trimmed. His nose was a little too hawkish for her taste, and his somewhat shaggy hairstyle could do with some attention. Still, she was intrigued by his profile, and what she could see of his features hinted of a sense of humor and a comfortable, friendly kind of strength.

She swallowed an embarrassed groan when he unexpectedly turned and looked directly at her. Mortified, she backed quickly away from the studio window, briefly registering the disappointing thought that he seemed markedly unimpressed; he hadn't blinked an eye when he caught her staring.

"May I help you, or are you just window shopping?"

Jennifer jumped again, choking off a yelp of surprise when a deep voice at her back halted her movement away from the studio. Flushed, she whirled around to encounter, almost nose-to-nose, a more conventionally handsome man than the disc jockey. This one was not so dark with sun-

10

burnished skin and sun-streaked blond hair. He wore a winter white ski sweater, and his green eyes danced with fun above a remarkably perfect nose and a dark mustache.

Jennifer was beginning to think she had somehow taken a wrong turn and ended up in an employment agency for male models instead of a Christian radio station. She gaped at the life-sized physical fitness ad who was smiling all over his face at her.

"Help me?" she stammered in confusion. "No—I mean yes!"

The green eyes twinkled with even more amusement. "Yes, you need help, or yes, you're window shopping?" he teased. "Never mind—either way, I'm available. Well, not actually available, but certainly accessible."

Jennifer stared at him. Her recovery time was slower than usual this morning, probably due to the less than five hours sleep she had had the night before. "I . . . I have an appointment for an interview. With Mr. Kaine—"

"Aha! Then you must be Jennifer Terry." He offered his hand and continued to smile.

Jennifer adjusted her shoulder bag and drew a long breath of relief as she extended her hand. "Yes, I am."

He captured her hand and shook it vigorously. "Gabe Denton, Jennifer. News director, gofer, and court jester. At your service." He paused, then added, "You're a Buckeye, right?"

His smile was infectious, and she grinned back as she nodded. "Yes—Athens, Ohio. Is everyone in West Virginia this friendly?"

"You bet. It's the altitude. You went to O.U., didn't you?" Without waiting for her to answer, he continued to toss out words at an amazing rate of speed. "I almost went there, too, but Daniel talked me into West Virginia U. He's forever talking me into something. I have no backbone, I suppose."

Her mind reeling from his high-speed verbal barrage,

Jennifer replied weakly, "I see."

"I reviewed your resume with Dan last week. He's very interested. Come on, I'll buy you a cup of coffee while you're waiting for him. He'll be free in a few minutes."

He led her down a paneled hallway to the left of the studios, carrying on a constant flow of idle chatter. Turning, they then entered a bright, informal lounge where the whisper from a heat register was the only sound. It was a comfortable, cheerful room with hanging baskets placed here and there, a floral chaise and matching chairs. A large commercial coffee urn and a variety of cups rested on a white table.

"Did you drive down this morning?" Gabe asked, pouring a cup of coffee that smelled rich and delicious. Jennifer's stomach reminded her with a growl that, in her characteristic rush out of the house, she had skipped breakfast.

"Yes, I left home about seven."

"No one should have to get up that early on Saturday," he said with a sympathetic grimace. "It's criminal."

"Actually, I'm used to it," she explained, gratefully accepting the coffee. "I have to be at the station where I'm working now by six o'clock every morning except Sundays."

"No wonder you're job hunting." He extended a small plate of wafers to her, and she quickly took a couple. "Well, Jennifer, I hate to desert you, but I have an insurance rep in my office who's expecting a stroke of advertising genius from me. Do you mind waiting alone? I'll go in and tell Dan you're here."

After a quick sip of coffee, she motioned him on. "I'll be fine. Go ahead. Oh—and thanks for the coffee!"

"It'll be great working with you, Jennifer." He gave her a quick wave and turned to go.

"But I haven't got the—" She stopped, her words trailing him as he dashed out the door.

She carried her coffee over to a large window, thinking

that if the lounge were indicative of the rest of the station, the place was definitely a step up from the small Christian station where she worked now. It was little more than a two-room warehouse a few miles outside Athens.

She liked the job, but the time had come to move if she were ever to make a dent in the loan her dad had assumed for her music studies in Italy. The salary quoted for this position was surprisingly good. It was the primary reason she hoped to make a memorable impression upon Daniel Kaine.

Not for the first time, Jennifer wondered what to expect of the man who owned and managed the station. She already knew he was young. She remembered what Dr. Rodaven, her former professor at Ohio University, had told her when he first contacted her about the job.

"I've only met the man twice, Jennifer, but I was impressed with him. He's in his early thirties. Seems highly intelligent—a fine Christian, too, by the way. I don't suppose you'd remember, but he made quite a name for himself and his community several years ago in the Olympics. He must have taken at least two, maybe three, gold medals in swimming. I watched him on television—a real powerhouse in the water. Great athlete. A terrible tragedy, what happened to him . . . "

"What do you mean? What happened?"

"He's blind. There was a car accident a few years ago—a teenager, I think. Drunk. Daniel Kaine lost his sight, and I believe the boy died."

She had nearly backed off then and there. A man with that kind of handicap might be expecting someone to function more as a personal secretary than an executive assistant. What Jennifer really wanted was to break into management and perhaps have a show of her own. However, the stark reality of financial need was enough incentive to lure her to Shepherd Valley for an initial interview.

So, here she was, though not without reservations. She sipped the hot coffee slowly, moving to the other side of the room so she could gaze out at the winter landscape.

I could learn to love this place in no time, she thought. *Just look at those mountains.*

Shepherd Valley was a valley in the truest sense of the word. A town of approximately thirty thousand people, it nestled peacefully at the bottom of a wide range of some spectacular mountains, white now with January snow. The entire community formed an oval, with only a few buildings fanning out into the surrounding woodsy area. Since the radio station sat squarely on top of a hill, Jennifer had a breathtaking view of the Appalachian settlement below. It appeared to be very old and quaint and tranquil.

Her thoughts returned to Daniel Kaine. The only blind person she had ever known was Miss Rider, the elderly piano teacher she'd seen for half an hour weekly while she was still in elementary school; she barely remembered her. What was it like, living without sight, knowing you'd never see again? For, according to Dr. Rodaven, Kaine's blindness was permanent, caused by severe damage to the optic nerve.

Jennifer shuddered, trying to imagine how she would deal with a tragedy like that in her own life. *How would you ever learn to live with it?* Her mind went briefly to her younger brother, Loren, a victim of cerebral palsy. She felt the sharp twist of pain that unfailingly accompanied any thought of the copper-haired youth she had helped to raise after the death of her mother. Which would be worse, she wondered, spending your life in a wheelchair or living in continual darkness? She pressed her lips together, resolutely swallowing a familiar lump of resentment.

But she couldn't stop thinking about Daniel Kaine. Always curious, she turned and placed her nearly empty coffee cup on the white lacquered table beside the chaise. She shut her eyes and stood perfectly still for a moment to fix her sense of direction. Then, slowly and cautiously she began to walk across the room, her hands flailing out and groping with every step. She felt something fall with a soft thump but refused to give in to the temptation to look. Weaving back and forth, she continued to walk. She flinched when she heard something else topple, but still resisted the urge to open her eyes.

I should be close to the door by now, she thought. She turned sharply to retrace her steps—and collided so soundly with a hard, massive shape that her head snapped backward from the unexpected blow.

Her eyes flew open to encounter an incredibly broad chest encased in a crimson V-neck sweater—a chest her hands were now braced against in an attempt to steady herself. *The disc jockey!* she realized with a sinking thud in her stomach.

Miserably, she raised her eyes upward, then higher still, to the dark, bearded face lowered toward her with a questioning stare. *Oh, no,* she thought sickly, *there really is such a thing as "Capri blue eyes!"*

The voice was low, richly timbred and very smooth with a soft but definite drawl. The description "mellow velvet" swept briefly through Jennifer's mind.

"Excuse me. Am I, ah . . . in your way?"

She uttered a little sound of embarrassment. "Oh—no! I—oh, I'm *so sorry!"*

The big man smiled, and Jennifer had a fleeting, irrational thought of a sunrise she'd once seen from her window in Rome—slow and gentle and breathtaking.

"Did I run into you? Or did you run into me?" He laughed easily and continued to stare down at her with those wonderful eyes that galvanized her entire nervous system.

Startled, she realized that her hands were still pressed against him. She yanked them abruptly away with a choked exclamation. "I—I definitely ran into you!" she stammered. "Did I hurt you? Oh, I feel so incredibly *stupid!"*

Still smiling, he braced one arm above her on the

doorframe, trapping her within his space. "Don't. I run into things all the time."

He was being wonderfully nice, but she felt like such a klutz! She could have kicked herself. Here she was, face to face with the first man to ever make her heart tumble over itself—*and I'm walking around with my eyes closed, falling into things, for goodness' sake!*

"I'm not totally crazy, honest! You see, I have an appointment with Mr. Kaine for a job interview, and . . . well, I was waiting for him, and I started thinking about what it would be like, not being able to see, you know? And I—well, I just shut my eyes to try it out for myself, and—oh, I suppose it *sounds* even more stupid than it must have *looked!*"

She knew she was chattering—she always did when her composure was threatened—but the disc jockey simply kept on smiling, as though he didn't quite know what to make of her.

Running his hand lightly over his beard, he finally spoke. "I don't think that's so stupid," he drawled softly. "In fact, I think it shows a lot of sensitivity."

"You do?" She stared at him blankly.

He nodded. "Absolutely. You were wondering what it's like to be blind, right?"

"Yes. But my brother told me I should say 'unsighted' rather than 'blind,' that it's more current. What does Mr. Kaine prefer, do you know?"

He appeared to consider her question carefully for a moment. "Ah—I don't think he much cares what you call it. So . . . you have an interview for a job here?"

"Yes, as Mr. Kaine's executive assistant. Have *you* been here long?"

"Mm-hm. A long time. You any good?"

"I beg your pardon?"

"At what you do. Are you good?"

Really, wasn't he *strange*? "Well, I think I am. I have a

16

degree in broadcast communications and experience. What do *you* do?"

His smile was disarmingly boyish. His even white teeth flashed in dazzling contrast to his dark hair and skin. Moving away from the doorframe, he took her hand and placed it firmly on his forearm, covering it with his much larger, darker hand as he urged her through the doorway.

"As a matter of fact, I own the place, Jennifer. Jennifer Terry, isn't it?" he said smoothly as they entered the connecting office.

"Now then, why don't you just come in and sit down, so we can talk. I've got a hunch you're already hired, so we'd better start getting acquainted, don't you think?"

2

Jennifer skidded to a dead stop on the other side of the door, narrowly avoiding a second collision with the man. Her mouth fell open on a sharp intake of breath, and she gaped at him in startled silence. He waited, a trace of mischief scurrying across his features.

"*You're* Daniel Kaine?"

"Guilty." The man had a grin like a jolt of electric current.

She didn't know whether to groan with embarrassment or simply try for a fast getaway. "Well, if you'd only *told* me—" she muttered weakly.

"Told you?"

"Who you *are!*"

He nodded. "Sorry. I guess I got a little . . . sidetracked."

"Well, now that you've seen me make an utter spectacle of—" She slapped the palm of her hand against her head, moaning softly when she realized what she'd said.

"I wasn't looking—honest." A dry note of amusement edged his words.

"I'm so sorry," Jennifer said miserably, wondering if she would have liked the job.

"Jennifer—sit down and relax, okay?"

His hand still covered hers on his thickly muscled forearm, and he pressed it gently, moving her across the plush, sand-toned carpet to a leather chair that sat directly opposite a large walnut desk.

Jennifer sat down cautiously, perching herself on the edge of the chair. Glancing up, she encountered the curious, dark-eyed gaze of one of the most beautiful dogs she'd ever seen. An elegant golden retriever resting casually beside the massive desk studied her with friendly interest.

Her embarrassment was momentarily forgotten. "What a lovely dog!"

"Ah . . . she likes to hear that, don't you, girl?" Easing his large frame onto the chair behind the desk, Kaine leaned sideways to stroke the dog's head affectionately. "Jennifer, meet Sunrise Lady of Shalimar. Her friends call her 'Sunny.' "

"Is she—"

"My guide dog," he finished for her. "One of the best—from the Seeing Eye in New Jersey." He skimmed his hands quickly over the right side of the desk top, stopping when he touched a slim manila file folder. Opening it, he began to run his fingertips lightly across the Braille letters of the top sheet.

The dog sat up on her back legs, tilted her head to the side and began to whine softly. "I believe Sunny would like to introduce herself to you," Kaine said, smiling as he continued to read the Braille file.

"Is it all right to pet her?"

He nodded. "It's fine when she isn't working."

Jennifer extended her hand and the retriever immediately perked up her ears even more, then looked appealingly at her owner.

As though he could see her bid for approval, he inclined his head slightly. "Go on, girl."

Sunny shook off her dignified demeanor at once, bounding over to Jennifer and pressing her head into her lap in an undisguised attempt to get her ears rubbed. Jennifer complied, laughing at the small sounds of pleasure coming from the dog's throat. "How old is she?"

He thought for a moment. "A little over seven. But she thinks she's still a puppy."

He called the retriever back to his side, and she returned without hesitation.

"Okay, Jennifer, I think I remember most of the information on your resume. Gabe went over it with me a few days ago." He leaned comfortably back in his chair and locked his hands behind his head. "You're twenty-seven?"

Jennifer nodded, then caught herself and spoke. "Yes."

"Born and raised in Athens, Ohio. Nice town," he said thoughtfully. "I was there two or three years ago with my teen ensemble. I noticed Carey Rodaven was one of your references. Did you study with him at O.U.?"

He continued to mix his questions with casual, friendly comments for the next few moments. Jennifer was intrigued by the slow, rambling way he spoke. His words flowed smoothly in a soft Appalachian drawl. As she listened to his mellow voice, she scrutinized his features.

If you could accurately measure a person's character by his face, she would judge Daniel Kaine to be an extremely kind, good-natured man who had known more than his share of trouble, yet come through it reasonably unscathed. Everything about his appearance, his voice, his mannerisms seemed to fuse together in a unique combination of unshakable strength, patient tolerance, and relentless humor.

He also possessed, she thought uncomfortably, a distinct magnetism. His size, rather than presenting the blustering threat of an aggressive male grizzly, was more the endearing appeal of a comfortable but powerful Gentle Ben. He appeared to be essentially pleasant; she would guess him to be a man who seldom lost his temper. In addition, something in that youthful, mischievous grin told her he probably liked to have fun and might even be a bit of a tease.

But he also had a blunt, no-nonsense way about him that unnerved her. He was direct in a manner that gave Jennifer the disquieting conviction that Daniel Kaine would be impossible to mislead. She suspected that he possessed the intuitive ability to go straight to the heart, to strip aside any superfluous layers of camouflage and pierce the depths of another's spirit.

It didn't help that his thickly lashed blue eyes—beautiful eyes, Jennifer thought—although sightless, followed sound and movement and contributed to the overall impression of a highly developed intelligence and sensitivity. It was true that they lacked perfect focus, but this simply had the effect of giving him a somewhat pensive expression, as though he were continually looking at or listening for something in the distance. When he faced her, Jennifer had the sharp, uncomfortable sensation that he could *see* her.

His words jolted her back to attention when he put her file aside and leaned forward, lacing his fingers together on top of the desk. "Why don't I fill you in on the job first, Jennifer; then, if you're interested, I'd like to hear more about you." He smiled again, seemingly intent upon putting her at ease.

"About the job description that was sent to you—it might have been a little vague," he continued in his soft, mild voice. "What I'm looking for is someone to function as an assistant station manager as well as my exec. Gabe Denton, the comedian you met earlier, has more to do than he can handle. He's our program director and acting sales manager and—well, I've just got to get some help for him. There's a fellow coming in next week to interview for sales manager. If he works out, that will help, but we still—"

The telephone interrupted him with a shrill ring, and Jennifer glanced at the special instrument with its large, raised numerals as he lifted the receiver. "Sorry—my secretary doesn't work on Saturday, so I have to pick up my calls. I'll try to make it quick."

Resisting the urge to study him while he was on the phone—somehow it seemed unfair, almost as though she'd be taking advantage of his handicap—Jennifer let her gaze roam over his desk. A large Bible, probably Braille, she

21

thought, lay close to his right hand, and just a few inches away stood a clock with raised numerals and a machine that looked like a small record player. To his left was a green, somewhat battered IBM electric typewriter, as well as numerous papers with the raised dots she knew to be Braille. There was another machine, unfamiliar to her, that looked like a small typewriter. Bookshelves held a state-of-the-art stereo system and on the opposite wall were framed photographs of Christian recording stars. Many of the photos, Jennifer noted with interest, included Daniel Kaine in various poses with the performers.

She was trying not to eavesdrop, but when she heard the agitation in his voice and saw his heavy dark brows knit into an annoyed frown, she couldn't help but wonder what was so disturbing about the telephone call.

"Listen—" The soft, gentle drawl she'd found so charming moments before had deepened and now sounded almost gruff. "I don't know what your problem is, but you're not going to solve it like this. If you want to come in and talk, that's fine, but—"

Surprised by his abrupt change of manner, Jennifer was even more puzzled when she heard a loud click at the other end of the connection and saw Kaine hold the receiver away from his ear. He replaced it slowly and quietly, shaking his head from side to side in puzzlement. He managed a brief smile for her before he spoke. "Takes all kinds, I suppose." He made no attempt to explain what had transpired, and Jennifer didn't ask.

"So . . . where was I? Ah—I was interested in the job you're doing now, Jennifer. Gabe said you have quite a variety of responsibilities, that you're doing a little of everything."

Again she nodded in reply, then quickly corrected herself. "Yes, it's just a small station. Everyone has to be a jack-of-all-trades."

"Well, that could be a real plus around here," he said.

22

"Things get kinda wild every now and then. It would help to have someone who could pitch in as needed." He leaned forward a little more.

"Let me explain something else before we go any further, all right?" His pleasant, good-natured smile was back to normal now. "Some people are intimidated by my handicap. They simply can't relate to it, so they find it next to impossible to work around me. That makes it difficult for me, too. I've got to have someone in this job who isn't going to get all strung out about working with a blind man. Someone who'll be comfortable with me—so I can be comfortable, too. We're going to be together too much for it to work any other way. Do you understand what I mean?"

She considered her answer for only an instant. "I think so. And I've got to be honest with you, Mr. Kaine. I've never worked with anyone . . . who can't see. But I don't think it would be a problem for me once I learned your way of doing things."

He nodded slowly, running the palm of his hand lightly across his beard. "Well, let me put your mind at ease about one thing. If you're afraid you'd end up as a nursemaid, you wouldn't. Most things, I do for myself. My little blonde here," he leaned over to stroke the retriever behind her ears, "gives me a lot of independence I wouldn't have otherwise. And Katharine Chandler, my secretary, keeps me more organized than I'd like to be. I'm sorry you couldn't meet her today; she puts in so many hours through the week, I don't think it's fair to ask her to come in on Saturdays, too."

He crossed his arms over his chest, and the powerful set of his massive shoulders reminded Jennifer that the man had been an Olympic swimmer. She had to force her attention back to his voice.

"I have a housekeeper to keep my place from turning into a condemned area. And I also have an over-protective sister who takes care of my social life—such as it is." He flashed his

23

annihilating grin and pushed his chair even further away from the desk.

"And, of course, I have Gabe." A flash of humor darted across his face. "He's my right hand. And my best friend. He's also the best program director a station could find. His sense of humor leans a bit to the odd side every now and then, but he's a great guy. He's also my part-time chauffeur, and drives me to and from the station every day. Anyway, I've got all the personal attention I need—sometimes more than I can handle. What I *do* need is an assistant with some smarts and a healthy dose of common sense who can also take my blindness in stride." He paused for just a moment, then asked, "You're a Christian, aren't you, Jennifer?"

"Yes, I am," she answered quickly.

"Everyone who works here is," he told her. "We try to function primarily as a ministry. 'Course, we have to make a profit to pay the bills, but we try to keep the priorities straight. Did you grow up in the church?"

"Yes. My grandfather was a minister. In fact, he started the church my family attends."

He nodded. "With your background in music, I imagine they keep you real busy singing."

Jennifer swallowed hard, not answering for a moment. When she finally spoke, she deliberately kept her tone even and bland. "Actually, I don't sing anymore."

He raised one dark brow inquiringly. "Not at all?"

"No."

She waited tensely for the question he seemed about to ask, but he simply smiled after a brief hesitation and changed the subject. "Well, now it's your turn to ask questions."

Relieved, Jennifer leaned forward a little. "What exactly would my responsibilities be?"

He lifted a hand with an encompassing motion, then leaned back in his chair and stretched his arms behind his head. "Helpin' me run the place, mostly. You'd coordinate programming with Gabe, do some p.r. for us, cover a lot of the community stuff—you know, concerts, church activities, civic meetings, all that sort of thing. I said you wouldn't be a nursemaid, but you *would* be driving me around a good bit, I'm afraid. Would you mind that?"

"Not at all," she answered quickly, surprised to realize that she found the idea rather appealing.

"Good. I'd need you to get going on one thing right away. We're the coordinating station for a nationwide radiothon coming up in just a few weeks. Gabe and I have been working on it for months, but we keep getting bogged down in other stuff. Consequently, we're nowhere near as far long as we should be with the planning for this thing."

"What kind of radiothon?"

"We hope to accomplish two or three things in regard to getting stronger drunk driving laws. We want to educate the public, get them behind it. Too many people are still ignorant of the statistics and the lousy laws we're dealing with. We need to generate more public awareness, more financial support, and more political pressure to get things done." He hesitated a moment, then went on. "I was asked to coordinate it because of my own experience. My blindness was caused by an automobile accident—the boy driving the other car was drunk."

He said it calmly and matter-of-factly, obviously expecting no response. "I suppose I should warn you, Jennifer," he continued with a smile, "that you'd probably have to put in quite a few weekends and evenings. But I'd make it up to you. You could have time off through the week every now and then. By the way, do you like to jock? Would you want a show of your own?"

"Actually, that's one of my favorite parts of the business," Jennifer admitted quickly, by now keenly interested in the job.

"Well, you could have your choice right now between two

shows. I need someone for a live talk show in the evening, or you could have a three-hour drive in the afternoon."

Jennifer was hooked. "I think I'd really like the job, Mr. Kaine."

"The name's *Dan*, okay? You've got a dynamite voice, Jennifer, you know that? Should be great on the air."

Before she could reply, he went on in his slow, soothing drawl. "Can I ask you about something else? Gabe filled me in on most of your background, but I've got to admit that I'm curious about how you went from studying opera in Rome to a radio station in West Virginia." He hoisted one large, tennis-shoe clad foot to the desktop.

"I—well, it's kind of a long story." She was deliberately evasive, hoping he wouldn't press her for details.

"That's all right," he said agreeably, looking as though he had all the time in the world.

She swallowed with difficulty, feeling her stomach knot with tension. The memories were still painful—too painful to discuss with a stranger, even one who seemed as kind as Daniel Kaine. "Mr. Kaine—Dan—I don't think it's relevant. And it is . . . personal."

He looked surprised, but recovered quickly. As though he had no intention of retreating from the subject, he tried again. "Your sheet said you'd studied voice for a long time. Two years in Rome with some famous *maestro*, right? Then you came home, went to O.U. for a degree in communications, and worked in a radio station on the side." He paused, but only for an instant. "You were interested in a stage career in opera?"

"I . . . was at one time, yes."

"Why'd you change directions?"

After a noticeable hesitation, Jennifer answered quietly, her tone flat and unemotional. "Because I wasn't good enough to do what I had originally hoped to do."

He tapped his long, blunt fingers lightly on the desk. "Who said?"

She made a weak attempt at lightness. "One of the best voice coaches in Europe. He said it very kindly, of course."

Picking up a pencil, Kaine twirled it back and forth between the thumb and two fingers of one hand. "That's rough. Is that what you'd always wanted, to have an operatic career?"

Jennifer nodded, again forgetting his sightlessness. She blinked furiously against the hot wetness burning her eyes. Impatient with herself and unsettled by his apparent determination to press the issue, she remained silent, even though he was obviously awaiting some sort of reply from her.

After an awkward silence, he went on. "The pain's still pretty fresh, is it, Jennifer?" he questioned softly.

If she admitted the truth she'd feel foolish. It sounded so petty contrasted to the enormity of his problem. Her own loss suddenly seemed pathetically insignificant as she studied him. She wondered at his air of self-assurance, his apparent tranquility. It had to be a front, she told herself defensively. No one with that kind of handicap could possibly be as emotionally . . . *together* as he appeared to be. No, she concluded abruptly, either Daniel Kaine was some sort of a rare spiritual giant or he had simply erected one of the most impressive facades she'd ever encountered. Her instincts strongly favored the latter. At any rate, she felt a grudging touch of respect for him.

Once more he met her silence with the same easygoing, pleasant tone of voice. "So this job is what? An alternative?"

"Yes," she replied tersely. "An alternative."

To her surprise, he smiled. "You want it just for the money?"

Jennifer had always found it impossible to be less than honest. Lifting her head somewhat defiantly, she admitted, "That's the biggest reason, yes. My father mortgaged almost everything we have to send me to Italy. I have two younger brothers—one who just married and another . . . in a private school. It's time I paid my own way."

"I can understand that," he said agreeably, still smiling. "What about moving? Would that present a problem for you?"

So he hadn't written her off after all! He was actually considering her for the job. "No, it wouldn't," she said quickly. "My only ties are my family—and I wouldn't be all that far away from them, just a few hours. And, Mr. Kaine—Dan—what I said about the job being an alternative . . . I'd still do my best for you, I honestly would."

His smile grew even warmer, and his voice held a note of interest when he spoke again. "You're not intimidated by me—by my blindness—are you?"

"I—" She stopped, considering his question. "No. No, I don't think I am."

With one last tap of his fingers on the desk, he rose from his chair and walked slowly around to her, extending his hand, which she took as she stood up. "I thought not. Well, we need to see about finding an apartment for you. Will you need a furnished one or unfurnished?"

He was offering her the job! Just like that! She lifted her face to his and smiled brightly, forgetting that he couldn't see her appreciation. "Furnished. And cheap."

He grinned. "We'll get Gabe and my sister, Lyss, to help us with that. Lyss is coming over to go to lunch with us in a while; we can talk to her about it then. How soon do you think you could start, once we find you a place to live?"

"Two weeks?"

"Great. I'll call Gabe in a minute and see if Lyss is here yet."

For an instant, he appeared to consider something. Then, his expression briefly uncertain, he dipped his head down. "Jennifer?" His voice was soft and halting. "I wonder—would you be offended if I . . . looked at you? With my hands?"

28

Something caught and tightened in Jennifer's throat, but she ignored it. "No—I mean, I don't mind at all."

It was an unsettling experience. She hadn't expected such gentleness, not from such a big man. He rested his hands lightly on her shoulders for just an instant before moving to trace the oval of her face, hesitantly at first, then with more confidence. He molded her face between his large hands, shaping every feature with light but firm strokes.

"You're tall. What . . . five-seven?"

"Eight," Jennifer said tightly, clearing her throat. "Five-eight, actually."

He nodded and smiled thoughtfully. "That's good. Short girls make me a little crazy. I never seem to be able to find 'em, you know? Never know how far down they are."

Jennifer stared blankly into his face, then laughed, but only for a moment. So unexpectedly intense was her response to his touch that she had to close her eyes against it. His fingertips were heavily calloused, and she fleetingly wondered what sort of work a blind man would do to cause callouses. His hands explored slowly, brushing over her high forehead, lightly winging out from her large, dark brown eyes, barely touching her closed eyelids, seeming to take note of her thick lashes before moving down over her high, prominent cheekbones and the sunken hollows beneath. He allowed his thumbs to touch the outside corners of her rather wide mouth only briefly, but long enough for her to catch a sharp, uneven breath before he fanned his fingertips gently along her jawline.

"I don't think you eat very much, Jennifer," he said softly, smiling as though he had discovered a small secret.

"My youngest brother calls me 'Bones,' if that tells you anything," she volunteered, thinking her voice sounded terribly unnatural. She thought she'd choke when he touched the dimple in the middle of her chin, then slid his hands slowly outward to scan the length of her long, thick

29

hair. He murmured something she didn't catch, then asked, "What color is your hair?"

"Uh . . . it's dark brown. With some red, auburn, I guess you'd call it," she added, hoping he couldn't detect the slight tremor in her voice.

"Must take forever to get it dry," he commented with a small, thoughtful smile. He moved one finger back to the pale scar just in front of her right ear. "What happened here?"

She could hardly believe the sensitivity of his hands. That scar was barely noticeable even to her. "I fell off a horse at a girlfriend's farm when I was about twelve. A piece of barbed wire fence got in my way."

"Tomboy, huh?" he chuckled softly.

"I'm afraid so." She wondered if the jelly sensation in her knees was due to lack of sleep or his touch.

His hands quickly framed her face once more, very gently, then dropped away. "Thank you, Jennifer, for understanding my need to do that." His features softened even more. "Gabe told me you were lovely," he said very quietly, with a nod of agreement. Then he grinned. " 'Bones,' huh? Sounds like something I'd say to *my* sister."

By the time Jennifer left for home late that afternoon, promising to return in two weeks, she had met Dan's sister, Lyss, who was a physical education teacher at the same Christian school she, Dan and Gabe had once attended. Along with Gabe, they helped Jennifer find and rent a delightfully furnished, three-room bungalow from "Papa Joe" Como, the owner of the restaurant where the four of them had lunch.

The quaint little house, decorated with white wicker furniture and cheerful, feminine prints, had once been a beauty salon. Papa Joe, who openly adored Daniel Kaine, appeared to be far more interested in a reliable tenant who would take care of his property than in charging an exorbitant rent. Jennifer was astonished at the monthly amount he quoted after learning that Dan had just hired her, and she quickly gave her new landlord a deposit for the first month.

When she was finally ready to leave, Dan walked her to her car, accompanied by Sunny. He leaned down to her window after she'd settled herself behind the steering wheel, and Jennifer again had the disturbing sensation that he was looking directly into her eyes.

"Well . . . hurry back, Jennifer," he said softly in a tone that sounded strangely reluctant. He touched her shoulder lightly, then straightened. "We'll have a welcome party for you once you get settled."

Watching him from her rearview mirror as long as possible—a tall, dark, enigma of a man with his golden companion standing quietly at his side—Jennifer felt the first trace of hopeful anticipation she'd known in years. She was surprised to realize that she wanted the next two weeks to pass quickly. Very quickly.

3

Dan walked into the kitchen of his house pulling a charcoal fatigue sweater over his head. Coming to a sudden stop, he pushed his hands deep into the back pockets of his jeans, and stood quietly, listening. To nothing.

For the first time in almost five years, he was engulfed by the same skin-prickling, blood-chilling sensation that had plagued him off and on during the early months of his blindness. The oppressive, menacing feeling that he was being watched—like a bug under glass. Isolated. Vulnerable. Helpless. Perspiration started on the palms of his hands and he felt the warning tremble in his arms and legs. His heart suddenly pumped harder, and he quickly touched one hand to the counter to steady himself from the slight dizziness he knew would follow. He tried to swallow but couldn't. All he could do was wait until it passed.

He'd hoped he was done with that, although his rehabilitation counselor in Pittsburgh had warned him that he could expect occasional anxiety attacks indefinitely. *It's these crazy phone calls,* he told himself. They were coming nearly every night now and sometimes through the day at the station. Rarely did the man say anything; usually the line remained ominously silent. Last night the phone had been quiet until long after midnight. When he'd answered, there had been nothing but the sound of ragged breathing.

Dan caught his own breath now, aware that his heartbeat was gradually slowing and leveling off. Feeling weak, he wiped his hands on his jeans and lowered himself to one of the stools at the counter to wait for his head to clear.

He knew he should tell someone about the calls. But he also knew what it would mean if he did. Everyone would start hovering over him again, watching him, *protecting* him. His mother, Gabe, Lyss—even his dad would get paranoid about it. It would be like before, right after the accident. He'd lose his freedom, his independence. *No.* Not yet. He was saying nothing until he absolutely had to.

What good would it do anyway? What could he tell them? *That some crazy keeps calling and hanging up? That the only thing he ever says is for me to mind my own business, to keep my nose where it belongs?* There had been no actual threat, although Dan had sensed a sick kind of anger and a near desperate urgency behind the voice the few times the man had spoken.

The dream was coming more often now, too. And it was different, more demanding, more harrowing than ever before. There was nothing he could do to prevent it. His subconscious seemed to have a will of its own and asserted it every few days, though he would routinely try to psych himself into avoiding the dream.

He would sleep uneasily, a sleep with no peace, just before finding himself on that same deserted, winding mountain road again, the road that was little more than a rough-hewn corridor gouged through ancient, craggy mountains. He would hang the corkscrew curve near the top of the hill only to be met by two blazing halos of light looming toward him through the fog on his side of the road. He would feel himself suspended, weightless, for a brief spark of eternity, just before the mushrooming headlights of the oncoming truck, like two furious, malevolent eyes, exploded into his face. Terror would grip him by the throat as metal rammed metal with a crunching thud and his body jolted and strained to burst out of the confines of the seatbelt, while glass shattered and blew to pieces in a slow-motion kaleidoscope of horror.

And then he would hear someone scream, not realizing it was his own voice until the smoking chamber of the car echoed the sound of it over and over again before tossing it out into the night, where it bounced across the mountain to be swallowed by the fog. Finally, he would gape through shock-glazed eyes at the last thing he would ever see in his lifetime, a face behind the windshield of the truck, a face fragmented and distorted by broken glass and a heavy shroud of mist. The face of fear, a macabre rictus, frozen in an endless, silent scream . . . .

And then the dream would end. Always at the same point, always in the same way, always incomplete. He would awake, at first in the eye of a storm of panic, then weary and drained with the reality that it was only a dream, that it was over . . . but that he was, indeed, blind. And he would lie quietly, perspiring and trembling, forcing himself to think about the dream, for there was always something unfinished about it, something he could never quite remember.

He supposed the calls could somehow be triggering a number of anxieties he'd had to deal with after the accident. He wondered, too, if there were any connection between the telephone calls and the upcoming radiothon. The station had recently begun to highlight the nationwide campaign with hourly announcements on the air, many of which Dan did himself. It wouldn't be the first time someone who was already a little unhinged went off the deep end because he didn't like what he heard.

With a resigned sigh, Dan straightened his shoulders and hauled himself to his feet. This was *not* the best frame of mind for the coming evening. He firmly willed himself to shake off the melancholy that had threatened to enfold his emotions most of the day, like a low-hanging cloud that refused to move.

Jennifer—and half the town, he reminded himself wryly— would be here within minutes. *Jennifer.* He said her name to himself, quietly, with a touch of a smile, relishing the sound of it on his lips. *You're in trouble, all right, buddy. But maybe not the kind you're worried about. The real trouble,*

I suspect, has a lot more to do with a certain lady who always smells like a vanilla-scented candle and has a voice like warm, thick honey bein' poured over marshmallows. The same lady who, according to Gabe, has exactly four freckles on her nose and looks like a model for a health food poster.

The lady also happens to be the guest of honor at the party you're hosting in a few minutes. He tried to shove his attention back to more mundane matters, but the thought of her presence in his home—an entire evening to simply be close to her, to hear that sensational laugh of hers, to fill his senses with the sunshine-warm fragrance of her heavy hair at his shoulder—made his smile break even wider across his face. He gave himself a mental shake of the head at his own adolescent foolishness, but the glow of his smile lingered.

With a self-mocking shrug, he pursed his lips in a soft whistle, palmed a few pretzels from a bowl on the snack-heaped harvest table in the dining area and walked into the living room. He went to stand in front of the fireplace, where gentle flames were rising and crackling cheerfully.

Sunny padded in and lay down at his side, tucking her toy rubber duck snugly between her two front paws. Dan dropped down to a squat on the hearth made of old street paving brick and began to stroke the golden, feeding her an occasional pretzel from his hand as he muttered a reminder to himself that "you must never spoil a guide dog, Mr. Kaine." *Absolutely.*

His shoulders flinched restlessly. He stood up and began to walk the length of the room, which in truth was a continuous number of rooms with no walls, an unbroken flow of colonial colors, primitive accent pieces, and early West Virginia carpentry. When he reached the "music room" at the far end of the first floor, he stopped to drop a cassette tape into a player on the bookcase shelf. Jerking the volume control well past the comfort level, he shoved his hands into

35

his pockets, broke into a satisfied smile, and started to sing along with a popular contemporary Christian band.

Sunny reluctantly stirred and raised her head to cast a long-suffering, mildly censuring look at him, as though to make the observation that he was turning more and more peculiar lately.

Less than a mile away, Jennifer spilled her cologne for the third time and took a long, disgruntled look at herself in the oval vanity mirror. "What is *wrong* with you tonight, klutz? You'd think you had a date at the governor's mansion."

Rummaging through several yet to be unpacked boxes, she found the pigskin boots she'd bought on sale the winter before and hurriedly put them on. She frowned at herself again in the full-length mirror on the bedroom door, deciding too late that the pleated slacks and paisley megajacket made her look even thinner than she was. She buttoned one large button, considered the effect, then immediately unbuttoned it, mumbling a short sound of regret at the thought of all the meals she'd skipped during the hectic days of packing and moving.

Raking a brush through her heavy hair, she suddenly paused with her hand suspended above her head. "Flash, kiddo. You do realize, don't you, that the one person you're so anxious to impress can't even see the result of your efforts?"

"Brilliant, Jennifer," she said under her breath, grabbing her shoulder bag and slinging it over her arm. "Nothing short of brilliant."

She shrugged quickly into her corduroy trench coat and began to fish for her car keys as she raced out the door. Tripping on the front step, she choked with exasperation when she dropped her purse upside down, spilling its considerable contents all over the small cement porch. She scrambled to pick up everything she'd dropped, shoving a collection of eight or nine pens and pencils back to the bottom of the bag, along with her wallet, a memo pad, half a dozen stamps, two Hershey bars—but no keys.

Irritation scraped at the back of her neck as she walked into the carport. A quick glance through the window of the car confirmed that the keys were still in the ignition. *At least, I didn't lock the car door,* she thought with grudging relief. *I have to stop living this way, I really do. I've simply got to get myself organized, get control of my life, establish a routine . . .*

She drove with extreme caution, deliberately holding in check the heavy foot her dad often accused her of having. The streets were little more than mounds of drifted snow and thin layers of ice. The fast-falling, wind-driven snow that had begun in the afternoon had stopped, but the road crews apparently hadn't been able to keep up with it.

In spite of a touch of apprehension about meeting so many new people all at once—the list Katharine had showed her earlier in the week looked as though Dan had invited most of Shepherd Valley—she was looking forward to the evening. She was curious about the way Dan lived and eager to see his home. At first she'd been surprised to learn that he lived alone and wondered how he could manage, even with Sunny. But after three weeks of daily contact with the man, she no longer questioned Daniel Kaine's ability to manage anything.

The light she'd been waiting for changed, and she moved through the intersection slowly, her mind still filled with thoughts of her enigmatic boss. There was no denying the attraction the man held for her, though she'd scolded herself more than once for the provoking way he'd come to occupy such a large segment of her thought life. She occasionally rationalized her response to him, telling herself that he was, after all, an intriguing, complex personality, far different from anyone she'd ever known. As for the way her emotions began to riot every time she came within a few feet of him—well, he was simply a very *compelling* man.

He was also a strangely *intimate* man, a trait that might have put her off in someone without Dan's innate kindness and acute sensitivity. But she'd quickly grown comfortable with his eagerness to know, to understand, to "see" through the eyes of others what he could no longer see for himself.

It was now routine for her to give him at least a sketchy idea of what she was wearing, especially color, to casually describe their surroundings when they were driving, to indicate to him any significant change in another employee's appearance, and to describe little things that caught her attention whenever they were together.

She had come to understand within a short time that he drew heavily upon visualization and considered himself fortunate in having been sighted most of his life. He had explained to her that he was still able to project images onto the screen of his mind, whereas those who had been blind from birth had to depend upon the observations of someone else plus whatever they could glean from their other senses to help them form mental pictures. Jennifer had said nothing, but she was highly skeptical about his positive attitude. She found it next to impossible to see even the smallest grain of "blessing" in the tragedy of Dan's blindness. Still, when she'd studied his face after he made the remark, she had been unable to see any trace of false courage or shallow optimism.

It would be difficult *not* to be drawn to the man, she insisted to herself once more as she turned slowly onto Keystone Drive. In addition to his commanding physical presence and multi-faceted personality, he bore his handicap with what Jennifer saw as an incredible maturity. Dan obviously relished his independence, yet he didn't hesitate to ask for assistance when he needed it. There was a definite aura of strength about him, but a touching vulnerability would occasionally surface when least expected.

As it had late that afternoon. She had walked into his office and found him standing at the large window behind his desk. His face and one hand were pressed to the glass as though he were staring outside.

His black hair fell, as usual, over his forehead on both sides, the silver streak barely brushing the vertical, pale scar at his eyebrow. He was wearing a white crewneck pullover with a quilted front and gray cords with worn knees. And he wore the casual outfit as he wore everything else—with the natural grace of an athlete who's comfortable with his own body. But there was a rare sadness imprinted on his features that tugged at Jennifer's heart. She felt a sudden intense need to say or do something that would bring a smile to his face.

She didn't speak, feeling awkward about intruding upon what was obviously an unprotected, private moment. But he knew she was there.

"Jennifer?" he questioned softly, without moving.

"Yes. I can come back—"

"No, it's all right," he assured her quickly, motioning her closer. "Come in."

She went to stand by him, seeing the vapor his warm breath had made on the cold windowpane.

"Katharine said it was snowing," he said quietly.

"Yes, it is. It started about an hour ago."

He rubbed his fingers gently against the glass, as though he could touch the scene outside. "I used to love to stand here and look down on the valley when it was snowing." His expression was pensive. "Do you like it—the snow?"

"Oh, yes. I love it! I always have."

He was quiet for a moment. Then he touched her lightly on the shoulder. "Help me see it again, Jennifer. Tell me what it looks like outside."

The wistful note in his appeal threw her off guard for just an instant. Swallowing with difficulty, she glanced from Dan's profile to the winter scene outside, forcing her voice into an even, conversational tone when she spoke.

"Well, let's see . . . it's dark, almost like evening. The street lights are on all the way down the hill—lots of houses are lit up, too. And most of the cars have their headlights on. It looks as if traffic's having a hard time already; I can see at least four or five cars stalled halfway up Rainbow Drive."

She stopped, moving closer to him to peer out the window. "It's a heavy snow. The branches on that old blue spruce by the walk are really drooping." Then, almost childlike, she added, as much to herself as to Dan, "The snowflakes are the big, fat squishy ones, the kind that are fun to catch with your mouth open."

She looked up at him, surprised to see that the melancholy that had darkened his features only moments before had now lifted and brightened to a sweetly tender smile of understanding. When he reached for her, fumbling to find her hand, she linked her fingers with his without thinking.

"Did your mom ever yell at you for messing up her window like this?" he asked, his hand pressing her index finger against the cold, wet glass in a faltering squeak as he prompted her to write . . . *J-e-n-n-i-f-e-r.*

"Now me," he suggested, still smiling as he transferred his hand from on top of hers to underneath it.

"Wait a minute—we ran out of steam," she laughed. "Blow."

"What?" He inclined his head, waiting.

"Blow on the window—we need more steam."

"Right. More steam." He pursed his lips to blow on the glass, then stopped. "Ah . . . tell me there's no one else in this room, Jennifer."

"Just us."

Leaning his forehead lightly against the glass, he quickly vaporized more of the window, and Jennifer then helped him write his name beneath hers.

"This is a very symbolic thing we've done here today, Jennifer. You realize that, don't you?" he asked gravely.

"Symbolic?"

"Absolutely," he assured her, dabbing his wet, cold finger on the end of her nose. "Once you write your name in a man's breath, you become a part of his life."

"Oh." The small sound was nearly lost as she swallowed with difficulty, reminding herself quickly that of course he was only joking.

Jennifer pulled her thoughts back to the present as she killed the motor of the car. Leaning back with a relieved sigh, she studied the "Kaine barn," Dan's home, about which she'd already heard a great deal. It was as unconventional and as unique as the owner. It truly *was* a barn—a large, restored early American barn attached to a small clapboard house, which, as Dan had explained to her, now housed his indoor pool. Structurally spectacular, it had a sturdy, rustic appearance with its dark oak siding, seam metal roof, and varied styles and sizes of windows. It was tucked into the hillside and looked down on the valley in what had to be, Jennifer thought, an absolutely breathtaking view.

She dragged in a deep, steadying sigh as she slid out from under the steering wheel and began to trudge up the snow-covered walk to the house. *Speaking of breathtaking views* . . . she muttered softly to herself. She stared for a long moment at the dark, bearded giant who had just thrown open the door and now stood waiting for her with a smile that made her heart go into an unexpected tailspin.

4

He dropped his hands lightly onto her shoulders as he helped her shrug out of her coat. "Relax, kid. Mountaineers are very friendly folks. You don't need to get tensed up about being in a room full of them."

Jennifer shook her head, marveling at his uncanny way of sensing her emotional barometer. "Nobody's ever given a party for me before. I'm a little nervous."

He squeezed her shoulders reassuringly and turned to hang up her coat, but Lyss walked up just then and did it for him. Jennifer stared at the two of them together, Lyss and Dan, struck again by how much one resembled the other. Lyss was tall, too, and as striking in her own way as Dan, with the same penetrating blue eyes and dusky dark hair that appeared to be trademarks of the Kaines.

Naturally, it wasn't long before Gabe joined them. Jennifer had observed that wherever Lyss was, Gabe was sure to follow. They were engaged—and had been, Dan had informed her, for nearly two years. Apparently Lyss was the holdout, insisting they have a down payment for a house before they married.

The four of them now started toward the kitchen but were stopped on the way by a small boy with silver-blond hair and polished-apple cheeks who came bounding up with Sunny at his heels. Dan grinned tolerantly and hoisted the boy up to his shoulder in one easy motion. "Did you and Jim give Sunny her dinner like I asked?"

"We put some good stuff in with her dog food, Dan. Hamburger and eggs." He gave Dan a hug and Jennifer a bashful smile.

Jennifer grinned at him. She had already met Jason Lyle

42

at church. The small eight-year-old with the enormous brown eyes was a mildly retarded orphan who lived at the County Children's Home. Both parents had been killed in a motorcycle accident when he was only a few months old. Dan had first become acquainted with the boy through the "Friend-to-Friend Association," a countywide mutual aid ministry for the handicapped which Dan and some people at his church had helped to establish. The Kaines and Gabe took turns seeing that Jason got to church and Sunday School each week.

He was an incredibly beautiful child, Jennifer thought, so physically perfect that it was difficult to realize he might never exceed the mental capacity he'd already attained. She could never be near the boy without feeling a stab of resentment at the cruel blow that had been dealt to him. How could God give a child such a wonderfully attractive appearance and then cripple his mind? Jason never failed to remind her of her younger brother, Loren, gifted with an unusually fine mind but a crippled body. To Jennifer's way of thinking, Loren and Jason were only two out of many examples of divine injustice.

She watched Dan swing Jason over his head and then set him lightly to his feet. There was an obvious flow of affection between the two of them. It was no secret around the station that Dan would like to adopt his little friend but was reluctant because he wanted more for Jason than what he thought he could offer as a blind, single parent.

"You go get Jim now and the two of you take Sunny outside for a few minutes," Dan instructed Jason. "And bundle up good, you hear?"

Jennifer watched the small boy trot off to the kitchen and begin to tug eagerly on Jim Arbegunst's sleeve. Jim, the tall, sad-eyed teenager she had first seen in the studio on the day of her interview, was helping Papa Joe with the food. Jennifer had been immediately drawn to this boy with his uncertain smile and haunted eyes. He worked part-time at the station after school and on weekends. Gabe often referred to him as "another one of Kaine's kids," because Jim routinely followed Dan around with undisguised devotion.

A quiet, noticeably unhappy youth, Jim was the only son of a farmer who lived on a small plot of land just outside of town, a piece of ground Dan described as too anemic to yield anything more than a token crop of vegetables. According to Dan, Caleb Arbegunst supplemented his income by running a temporary shelter for delinquent boys, a kind of stopping-off place where the court sent youngsters until more permanent arrangements could be made.

More than a few residents of the community, Dan had told Jennifer, were troubled by the shelter. From time to time questions were raised about the advisability of placing as many as half a dozen teens in the care of a man with Arbegunst's reputation. He was rumored to be an alcoholic with a fiery temper, and some believed that his wife, who had deserted Caleb and her son when Jim was still a toddler, had left because she could no longer deal with her husband's cruelty.

Dan's voice pulled Jennifer's gaze back to him. "My folks sent their best wishes—and their regrets that they couldn't be here," he said, moving Jennifer's hand to his forearm and covering it with his own as they began to walk through the house. "They won't be back from the convention until late tomorrow night. But they want you to come to lunch Sunday after church."

Jennifer had already been to Dan's parents' home twice for dinner and would have jumped at any invitation to enjoy Pauline Kaine's cooking again. "You're sure I won't wear out my welcome?"

"No chance. However, I *do* have an ulterior motive for getting you invited."

"Oh?"

"Mm-hm. I was wondering if you'd be willing to drive me up to the farm afterward. I should warn you, I suppose, that I'd like to take Jason along, too." He stopped walking and lifted his face slightly.

"The farm?" Jennifer was distracted by the music room at the far end of the house and the variety of instruments it contained. Her glance traveled over an ebony grand piano that occupied an enormous amount of space, a sophisticated synthesizer, a drum set, and a number of smaller, stringed instruments. In addition, the floor-to-ceiling bookshelves held an impressive stereo component system.

"Helping Hand—the place I told you about—the summer camp for handicapped kids." Located about sixty miles from Shepherd Valley, it had once been a conventional farm. For the last three years, Dan and Gabe had been working hard to turn it into a large camp that could accommodate children with a variety of handicaps.

"Oh—sure, I can go. No problem." Jennifer expelled a quick breath of surprise. "You never told me you were into music!"

He made a deprecating shrug. "I just play around with the keyboards some—it relaxes me. Mostly I use this stuff with my teen group. I like to have them out here to practice sometimes instead of rehearsing in the church basement. You'd be surprised at the cooperation I get when I promise a swimming party in exchange for a good rehearsal."

"I've heard a lot about your teen choir. How big is it?"

He grinned. "Don't ever let them hear you call them a *choir*, Jennifer. They're an *ensemble*, or a *group*, or even a *bunch*—but never, ever a *choir*. We usually have about fifteen. Ask me on a bad night, and I'd say fifty."

"And he loves every minute of it," added Lyss, who, along with Gabe, had followed them from the living area. "He and his drummer."

"His drummer? Who's that?" asked Jennifer.

45

"Who do you think?" asked Gabe, poking his head over Lyss's shoulder. "The kids call me *Sticks*."

"That's for your legs, man, not your drumming," Dan cracked, inclining his head toward Gabe.

"Uh, huh... well, you don't want to know what the little dears call you, old buddy," Gabe retorted dryly.

The three of them insisted on showing Jennifer the pool house—which was obviously Dan's special pride and joy. By the time they returned to the main living area, the house was swollen with guests milling about.

Jennifer spent the next half hour meeting people, then went upstairs to the loft with Lyss and Jason, who had had an accident with his fruit punch and was in need of a quick cleanup.

"This is where I sleep when I spend the night with Dan. I even keep some of my clothes here," the boy told her proudly as they entered the large master bedroom.

For an instant, Jennifer had the peculiar sensation that she'd just stepped onto a nineteenth century ship. The room held a variety of nautical items, including a splendid teak-and-brass binnacle and a hand-rubbed ship's wheel. The high, massive bureau was topped by a model of a clipper ship, and the wall shelves were lined with such artifacts as a whaling harpoon, different kinds of lanterns, a late 1800s compass, and a bell clock. The only things not directly related to the sea were the huge half-tester bed, covered with a colorful quilt, and a stone fireplace with an old, broad-bottom rocking chair in front of it.

Jennifer breathed a long, appreciative sigh. "What a *wonderful* room! Dan must love the sea!"

Lyss nodded as she scooped a clean shirt from a bureau drawer and helped Jason change. "He does. He and Gabe were always building ship models when they were kids. Before the accident they used to run white water on the Cheat every chance they got. He's always been crazy about water—anything from the ocean to a swimming pool." She

46

gave Jason an affectionate swat on the bottom and sent him on his way. He flashed Jennifer a mischievous grin as he raced by her and headed for the steps.

"The loft used to be just one big room," Lyss explained, gesturing to an open doorway opposite the bureau. "But Dan started doing so much counseling a couple of years ago that we partitioned off enough space to make a guest room for visitors."

"Counseling?"

Lyss took a moment to run a comb through her dark hair, glancing over her shoulder in the mirror at Jennifer. "Every now and then one of the therapists from the rehab center in Pittsburgh sends someone down here to stay a few days, someone who's having a hard time emotionally."

"I don't know how he does it," Jennifer said, shaking her head. "How does he keep up with everything? He must never have a moment for himself!"

"Well, he likes to keep busy. Sometimes I think he takes on a little too much, but—" She shrugged, leaving the thought incomplete.

"Lyss—how long did it take? For Dan to get over the accident?"

Lyss turned, pushed up the sleeves of her bright yellow sweater, and walked to a nearby window, glancing out for a moment. When she turned back to Jennifer, her expression was grave. "I'm not sure anyone ever . . . really . . . gets over something like that."

Feeling herself rebuked, Jennifer agreed softly. "It's just that he's so—" She groped for a word, finding none.

"I know." Lyss smiled a little and went to sit down on the bed, motioning for Jennifer to do the same. "It was difficult— horribly difficult—for a long time. Sometimes I didn't think he'd ever be himself again," she said quietly. For a moment her attention seemed to drift away as she plucked idly at the quilt.

"It's hard to imagine him ever being any different than he

is now," Jennifer said. "He has to be the most amazing man I've ever met."

Still not looking up, Lyss nodded and continued to smile. "He's pretty terrific." She ran her hand through her short, casually styled hair, then glanced across the bed at Jennifer. "He was such a great athlete. Did you know he took three golds at the Olympics? He's a marvelous swimmer! Of course, he's always excelled at anything he attempted—"

She stopped short and laughed. "Listen to me—I'm sorry. I'm afraid I'm not always very humble where my big brother is concerned."

"No, I understand," Jennifer protested. "You have every right to feel as you do about him."

"I *am* proud of him. I think he's wonderful," Lyss declared almost fiercely. "It was a nightmare, seeing him lose so much, watching him fight so desperately to hold on to his dignity—and his sanity. He had to start all over again, just like a child—" Her bright blue eyes glistened with unshed tears, and Jennifer impulsively reached across the bed to squeeze her hand with understanding.

"That's what was hardest for me," Lyss explained in a softer voice. "Seeing him so . . . defeated, so helpless. Dan's always been my hero; with six years between us, he spoiled me terribly the whole time I was growing up."

She was obviously remembering things she'd rather forget. "It was *awful*, seeing him like that, reduced to almost total helplessness. Watching him trip, bump into walls, stumble, having to stand by while he tried to feed himself without spilling—" She stopped, her voice again shaky. But she took a deep, steadying breath and continued, her expression brightening somewhat. "Of course, that was all before his rehabilitation, and Sunny. After he came back from Seeing Eye, he hired a therapist to give him special mobility training. It was amazing what he taught Dan in such a short time—how to arrange his clothing, how to code his money, organize the kitchen. He even gave him a crash course in self-defense."

"Without a doubt," she said, getting to her feet and walking around the bed toward Jennifer, who also stood, "his determination to be independent is one of the things that helped him make his way back after the accident." She attempted a smile. "Of course, that unbearable stubbornness of his may have been a factor, too. But over the long haul, it had to be his trust and his faith in God that helped him survive."

Jennifer's reply was faint. "I wonder how he did it." She glanced at Lyss. "How he managed to . . . go on trusting, under the circumstances?"

Lyss studied Jennifer, her blue-eyed gaze questioning but patient. "I don't think anyone but Dan could explain that," she said thoughtfully.

"Can I ask you one more thing—about the accident? What actually happened?"

"Oh, I thought maybe Gabe had told you, or even Dan. He'll talk about it, you know; you don't have to avoid the subject with him. Actually, what made the whole thing even worse for me was that Dan was on his way back from visiting me at the University the night it happened."

Her face briefly contorted with the pain of remembering. "It was my birthday, but I had finals and couldn't come home. So Dan drove down to deliver my birthday presents. He did that a lot. He'd just show up, with no warning. He would always bring me something, a new album or clothes or money." Her voice softened. "He was forever bringing me money. I always seemed to be broke when I was in college."

"And the accident happened on his way home?" Jennifer prompted gently.

Lyss nodded, leaning tiredly against the doorframe. "It was late, and there was a heavy fog." She swallowed with obvious difficulty. "It was a head-on collision."

"The other driver—he was killed, wasn't he?"

Again Lyss's eyes misted. "Yes. He was only sixteen. Apparently he was drunk—at least he'd been drinking a lot. The state police told us afterward the whole accident scene reeked of liquor. They said the boy had probably died instantly, even though Caleb ran for help as soon as he was able."

"Caleb?"

"Caleb Arbegunst. Jim's father. You see, it was his truck. The boy who was driving was one of the boys from the shelter. Caleb was bringing him back to his farm from the detention center, but he got sleepy and let the boy drive, not realizing he'd been drinking."

Her mouth twisted with disgust. "At least he *said* he didn't know. For my part, I wouldn't believe much of anything Caleb Arbegunst says."

"You know, I don't think I've heard a good word about that man in all the time I've been here," Jennifer said thoughtfully.

"And it's not likely that you will," Lyss said in an uncharacteristically grim tone of voice. "That's because no one can find anything good to say. Anyway, Caleb was thrown from the truck and was unconscious for a long time. When he came to, he went to a nearby farmhouse to call the state police. They found the boy dead and Dan unconscious."

An involuntary shudder gripped Jennifer for an instant. "And when he woke up . . . " she murmured to herself.

Lyss nodded and finished for her. "He was blind."

They were both silent for a long moment. Finally Lyss made a determined effort to smile. "Let's get you back downstairs. You're supposed to be the guest of honor at this shindig, remember?"

Later in the evening, about the time Jennifer would have

expected the party to break up, several people began urging Dan and Gabe down to the music room. Gabe pulled Lyss along with them, and she went to one of the synthesizers while Gabe sat down at the drums.

Jennifer watched the three of them with delighted surprise, her mouth dropping open when Dan crashed into a thunderous cadence at the organ, then unexpectedly broke away to the driving, contemporary beat of a well-known Christian number, one of Jennifer's favorites. Gabe immediately backed him up on the drums, and after the first few measures Lyss added the synthesizer—and her voice. She and Dan blended together in a tight, professional harmony. Almost instantly, everyone in the room became a part of the music by clapping their hands or singing along through a number of contemporary and traditional gospel songs.

Jennifer continued to gape with amazement at Dan. So he "played around with the keyboards a little," huh? She didn't try to analyze the warmth that enveloped her heart as she watched him, freely moving back and forth, grinning from ear to ear in unabashed enjoyment. She made the quick assessment that he could probably do anything he wanted at a keyboard. His voice was more than adequate, and she decided then and there that the man never seemed to run out of surprises.

The noise level in the room skyrocketed as Gabe plopped a green baseball cap onto Dan's head, then strapped an old flattop guitar around his neck. When Gabe reached back into the corner for a fiddle for himself, Lyss picked up a banjo—and everyone went crazy.

For the next twenty minutes, the trio indulged themselves in a bluegrass demonstration that left Jennifer wide-eyed and open-mouthed. She was astonished at the way Gabe could grind the fiddle, even more fascinated by Dan and his guitar as he turned it from a mournful, whining freight train one minute into a flashy, frenzied blaze of superior "pickin' " the next. Now she knew why his fingertips were so calloused.

At one point, she was caught short by an unexpected—and unwelcome—pang of yearning. Gabe jokingly called out to her that "this group could use a singer with a little class"—and for one precarious moment she was tempted.

It had been a long, difficult process, burying the desire to sing, a desire that at one time had been more powerful in Jennifer than the craving for food. But bury it she had. Or so she'd believed. Now here it was again, that aching, all-too-familiar pulsing in her veins that cried for an outlet. The need to create, to communicate, to celebrate—*No!* With a determination that bordered on anger, she slammed the door of her mind, shook her head at Gabe, and forced her attention to the trio a few feet away from her.

The three of them continued to ham it up to the hilt until Lyss gave up her banjo in defeat, collapsing in a fit of laughter at the slapstick antics of Gabe and her brother. Finally, as Gabe wiped his forehead on the sleeve of his bright green T-shirt, Dan tipped his baseball cap to the crowd, then tossed his arm around his friend's shoulder.

Jennifer stared at Dan, once more puzzling over his apparent contentment with life. Again she wondered how it could be genuine, yet she was more and more hard-pressed to doubt that it was anything but real. It was only lately that she'd begun to question her preoccupation with punching holes in what the man appeared to be. The possibility that had occurred to her was unsettling. In some inexplicable way, Dan stirred a sense of guilt in her that she was unwilling to face, as well as a longing that bordered on envy for whatever it was that gave his life such a unique, shining quality.

For Daniel Kaine was a man who lived his life in darkness—or, as he had recently corrected her, in grayness.

Because of his blindness, he walked among shadows, his steps guided only by his own personal faith. Yet he managed to shed a gentle, steady light on his surroundings, wherever he happened to be.

A sobering, distasteful thought had begun to whisper at her. A disturbing suggestion that perhaps she resented him, or at least resented his ceaseless passion for living, his freedom of the spirit, and his unfathomable—and, to Jennifer—inconceivable contentment and peace of mind.

Irritably, she wondered why she spent so much time thinking of him at all. Then she realized with a start that she had just asked herself another question she couldn't possibly—or wouldn't willingly—answer.

The truck was well-hidden in the thick grove of pine trees at the side of Kaine's house. He had parked just high enough on the first rise of the hill so he could see without being seen.

He could see everyone leaving now, laughing, calling back and forth to one another as they half-walked and half-slid to their cars. He'd been waiting for over two hours. It hadn't been so bad at first. As long as everyone was inside, he could run the engine and keep the heater going. But when they started coming out, he was afraid someone would hear the truck, so he'd killed the motor. Now he was shaking with the cold. He crossed his arms over his chest, hugging them to his body as tightly as he could, shivering even as his anger heated.

Must have had half the town in there. Big stupid deal. You'd think a blind man would be a little more serious-minded. But not Kaine. Oh, no, he wanted everybody to think he was no different from anyone else.

Like with the woman. He'd seen the two of them through the window, smiling at each other, mixing with the people just as though they were a normal couple, like they belonged

53

together. Was that grinning ape really dumb enough to think she liked him?

Everyone was gone now, everyone except for Kaine and the woman. He watched them coming out of the house. The dog was with them, but he wasn't worried about that. He was too far away to be noticed by the dog.

Kaine walked the woman to the car. As if he'd be any protection for her if she needed it. The man sneered through yellow teeth and rubbed his hands together to warm them. Even with gloves, they were stiff from the cold.

It wouldn't be long now, though. The woman was leaving. He cracked the window on his side just enough to listen. The light, steady wind carried their voices.

"What would it take to get you to sing again?"

She stared up at him. "I told you—"

"I know what you told me, Jennifer," he interrupted agreeably. "I'm just askin' if there's any chance I could change your mind."

"None." She paused. "Why?"

He pressed his lips together thoughtfully. "I'm going to combine the adult worship choir at church with the teens in an Easter cantata, a musical called *Daybreak*. We'll start on it soon. Having a trained voice like yours to sing the role of Mary Magdalene would be a real plus."

"You've never even heard me sing."

"You hum around the station all the time. Didn't you know that? I recognize quality when I hear it, kid."

"I—no. I'm sorry, Dan. I can't."

He nodded as if he understood, but then asked, "You wouldn't want to listen to it before you give me a definite no, would you?"

"Please . . . "

He looked for a moment as though he might continue to press. But instead, he smiled and touched her lightly on the arm. "Okay. Listen, you be careful on the hill. It's a lot worse

54

going down than coming up when it's icy."

The man in the truck winced and muttered an ugly sound when he saw the woman place her hand over Kaine's just before she opened the car door. "I'll be fine," he heard her assure him. "Dan—thank you for tonight. No one's ever done anything like this for me before."

Kaine dropped the retriever's harness, ordered the dog to stay, then placed his hands on her shoulders. *She oughtn't to let him touch her like that . . . she probably feels sorry for him . . . or aims to keep her job by playin' up to him . . .*

The man licked his lips, wishing he could hear what they were saying. But they were talking softer now, and the wind had shifted. *Was he going to kiss her?* He squinted, and his narrow green eyes turned even meaner.

No, she was getting in the car, starting the engine. Finally she pulled away and began to cautiously ease the car down the hill, leaving Kaine alone. Just him and the dog.

Suddenly the dog raised its head and turned toward the truck, lifting its ears in an alert, listening motion as a low, menacing growl started in its throat. Kaine jerked his head around, too, and for an instant the man in the truck froze in fear.

Then he remembered. Kaine couldn't see him. Kaine couldn't see anything. He grinned, stretching sallow, leathery skin over his cheekbones as he suddenly brought the truck's engine to life with a thunderous roar. He laughed to himself, a high, almost girlish sound as he came charging out from the grove of pine trees, heading straight for the blind man and his dog.

He saw Kaine's mouth drop open, saw panic wash over his face, and he laughed even harder. He floored the accelerator and crushed the heel of his hand against the horn, skidding away from the blind man at the last possible minute, only seconds before he would have leveled him. The dog went crazy behind him, snarling and barking like a wild thing.

Still laughing, he leaned on the horn again, then slowed and started down the hill like some sort of night monster making his way home after a bout of revelry.

That'll give him something to think about until I decide exactly how I want to finish him . . . when I'm ready . . . .

5

Ever since her welcome party three weeks before, Jennifer had been living in overdrive. She didn't mind; in fact, she thrived on it. The only thing that worried her was the extreme amount of time she seemed to be spending with Dan—more specifically, how much she *enjoyed* the time spent with Dan.

In addition to all the hours she was putting in on the radiothon, she now had an afternoon drivetime each weekday. She jocked her own show, consisting mostly of Christian contemporary and gospel music, public service announcements, and top-of-the-hour news. It was informal, fast-paced, and fun.

She was learning a lot and knew she still had a lot more to learn. Because most of the station's procedures had been adapted to Dan's blindness, she had to take a slightly different approach to a number of tasks she had once considered routine. With others, she had to start from scratch.

She had recently mastered his Braillewriter and could now type messages directly into Braille for him. Gabe had taught her how to make up the special, raised version of the "hot clock" he'd designed for Dan—a clever variation of the pie-chart broadcasting schedule used by sighted disc jockeys. By now she had met most of the station's major advertisers, covered an assortment of community events, learned her way around town, and done a fifteen-minute feature on Helping Hand Farm after her visit with Dan and Jason.

One of the things she enjoyed most was something for which she received no salary. Along with several other volunteers from the station and the community, she donated a few hours a week as a reader for the closed circuit radio service the station operated. The service provided over twenty hours of weekly broadcasting for the blind, furnishing receivers free of charge to those who couldn't afford to rent them.

In her spare time, she unpacked a box here and there. She was proud of the fact that after living in her little bungalow only six weeks, she had no more than four or five boxes left to empty. She was also making lists. This was part of her new strategy for organizing her life. She'd bought a book on creative self-organization at the bookstore in the mall and was following it chapter by chapter, line by line. She had noted that Dan was a very organized person, and, in order to maximize her efficiency as his assistant, she felt a need to follow his example.

Most of the time. At the moment, she was down on her hands and knees, burrowing about in the bottom of the credenza in her office. She was almost absolutely *positive* she'd put the entire stack of Braille scheduling charts for the radiothon in there. But she'd been so busy over the last few days, she'd taken to tossing everything that didn't require immediate attention onto the same shelf. Now the charts were missing—if they had ever been there in the first place.

She grumbled to herself, then scrambled to her feet and turned around to—"Dan! Don't *do* that!"

He stood by her desk, looking mildly offended. "What exactly did I do?"

"You—appeared. You're so incredibly quiet. Clear your throat or something when my back is turned—" She grimaced. "Oh, dear. I keep *doing* it! Of course, you don't know when my back is turned."

"Is your face red, Jennifer?"

"It certainly is. And so are my knees. I've been trying to find those schedules for the radiothon—the ones I typed on the

Braillewriter for you."

"They're on my desk."

"Why are they on *your* desk?"

"Didn't you say you typed them for me?"

"Yes, but I put them in my office—"

"No, you didn't. You put them on my desk." He shook his head sadly. "The mind is the first thing to go, kid."

"Not in my case. It's in better shape than my back."

"I have to go to the grocery today." He said it with all the enthusiasm of a man announcing the fact that he was facing an I.R.S. audit.

Jennifer perched on the edge of her desk and grinned at him. She found Dan's strong dislike for grocery shopping interesting and slightly amusing. He had been known to resort to trickery, even bribery, to wheedle someone else into doing it for him. He had successfully used his routine on Jennifer two or three times. *But not today, Daniel,* she thought impishly. *Not today.*

"Fine," she said evenly. "I'll be happy to go along and help, if you like."

He had been expecting just that response, obviously, and jumped on it. "You sure you have time?" Dan was a master of the thoughtful, concerned frown.

"Mm. No problem."

"I'm really pushed this afternoon. If you're sure you have time, I'll just give you my list. There're no more than half a dozen items on it." If a man's smile could be relieved, smug, and victorious all at the same time, Dan's was.

"No."

"No, what?"

"No, I'm not doing your shopping. I did it last week—twice. I said I'd *help*. Today, we go together."

He pulled his mouth to one side as if considering his chances. "Why together? It would be more efficient for only one of us to go, wouldn't it? It would certainly save some time." He arched one heavy brow in his best authoritative employer's expression.

"For you, maybe. Not for me. It'll be faster for me if you go along," Jennifer said brightly. "You say you need half a dozen items. Fine—I'll pick up three, you get the other three; we'll be back at the station in twenty minutes flat."

He slumped noticeably but accepted defeat gracefully. "You wanna go now?"

"After lunch."

"I suppose I'm buying."

"Why, what a nice idea, Dan! I'll be ready in five minutes."

After a quick lunch at Papa Joe's, Jennifer and Dan headed for the shopping center. A few minutes later she pulled off the road into the mall, splashing roughly through an enormous puddle. She squinted her eyes and peered outside the rainswept windshield of the car.

"What is this, monsoon season?" she grumbled. "Isn't there ever a happy medium in West Virginia's weather? Something a little less severe than blizzards and cloud-bursts?"

He shrugged. "We'll have snow again by the end of the week. Maybe sooner."

She glanced over at him. "And that's our radar weather exclusive for today, folks. News at eleven."

"I'm as accurate as that guy on cable, the one who rhymes all his forecasts."

"True. But he's a great looking guy."

"I would hope, Jennifer, that you're beyond being impressed by a pretty face."

"No woman can resist a true poet, Daniel."

"You actually watch that man?"

"Every evening at six. Faithfully."

He shook his head. "That's disgusting."

She grinned. "I'm going to let you and Sunny out at the

door while I park. Otherwise, you'll both drown."

She waited until Sunny had guided Dan through the entrance of the supermarket, then pulled away to look for a parking place. Finding nothing nearby, she nervously began to scout some of the rows farther away. It probably wasn't a good idea to leave him alone in the market too long, even with Sunny. He truly *did* get a little strange about shopping. She suspected he felt slightly less confident in stores than he liked to admit. Still, he *did* have Sunny, so he'd be fine . . . .

A few minutes later, Jennifer rushed into the supermarket wringing water out of her heavy, drenched hair. She stood near the checkout lanes and scanned the front of the store for a glimpse of Dan and Sunny, finally locating them at a nearby produce bin. She started toward them but stopped dead a few feet away from where they were standing, intrigued by the curious scene taking place.

Dan, a somewhat grim smile on his face, was attempting to separate one flimsy plastic sack from another. With a soft grunt of frustration, he finally dropped Sunny's harness, pulled open the sack, and began to sort through the oranges in the case, squeezing them lightly before dropping one into the plastic bag.

Jennifer was about to move and offer her help when a short block of a woman with square shoulders and white hair molded into individual pencil-width curls walked up to Dan. Her eyes were squinted in suspicious arcs as she peered up at him belligerently.

From her military stance at his right side, her head came only two or three inches above his waist. With a stern thrust of her chin, she gave a tug to her serviceable black raincoat and bellowed up at him in a voice that would have done a drill sergeant proud. "You shouldn't squeeze them oranges!"

Dan, his hand suddenly suspended in mid-air over the orange he was about to cup, cocked his head to one side quizzically, then bent down toward her voice. "Ma'am?"

His small, polite smile faded when she repeated her warning, with some elaboration. "You'll bruise 'em! You pick good oranges by their color, not by the way they squeeze. Here, let me show you."

With no further fuss, she tucked her red umbrella under one arm and planted herself firmly next to Dan as she began to sort efficiently through the oranges. "Hmph! Men! Reckon your wife's at work."

Too surprised to shift his usual sense of humor into gear, Dan simply stood alongside her, his mouth slightly agape. "Uh . . . ma'am—"

"Sent you to do the shoppin', did she? Well, you'd best go along with her a few times and learn how to do it proper! I wouldn't have turned my man—God rest his soul—loose at the market alone, not for anything, no sir! Look here, now!" She thrust a slightly mottled-looking orange directly upward to within an inch of Dan's nose. "See all those green places that're pushed in? You don't want that, no sir!"

Giving him no opportunity to react, she removed the bruised orange, trading it for a healthy one. "Here's a good one now. Well, open your *bag!*" Shaking her head with impatience, she plopped the large, perfect orange into the plastic sack still dangling from Dan's fingers. His mouth dropped open a little more, but he said nothing.

Jennifer chewed the knuckles of her fist in a noble attempt to choke off a giggle, willfully choosing to ignore the small voice that prompted her to interrupt.

"Well, are you gonna finish gettin' what you want out of that bin, young man? I have some shoppin' of my *own* to tend to!" She hurled a withering look of disapproval at Dan.

"Oh—sure . . . yes, ma'am!" In his haste to oblige, Dan knocked one of the largest, brightest oranges of the bunch from its fixed place on top of the rows. No less than twenty other round, ripe oranges promptly tumbled down and over the produce bin onto the floor.

Jennifer swallowed a groan of dismay and took a step forward, stopping again when Dan's adviser dropped quickly to her knees, hiking up her coat and dress enough to allow freedom of movement. Dan stood numbly mute, looking positively stricken.

"I swan, I don't know how some folks find their way home," his helper muttered, clucking her tongue with exasperation. She deftly rolled a few oranges up onto her arm, then proceeded to bob up and down like a tightly compressed jack-in-the-box until she'd replaced all the fruit in the bin. Waiting, Dan scratched his head, looked embarrassed, and reached for Sunny's harness.

Jennifer knew it was time to make an entrance. She fixed her expression in what she hoped was a sober appearance and approached the two of them. "Can I help?"

A quick look at Dan's scowling face confirmed what she feared—he'd heard the snap of amusement in her voice. In a tone thick with menace, he leaned over and growled at her. "Where'd you park—Cincinnati?"

"This your woman?" The steel-jawed fruit expert eyeballed Jennifer with disdain. "I'd handle the marketing myself, if I were you."

Jennifer swallowed almost painfully, halting the explosion of laughter that she knew would ruin her right there on the spot. "Ah . . . yes. Yes, I suppose I should," she said agreeably, smiling down at the frowning little woman.

After this exchange, Dan squared his shoulders with dignity, cuddled his plastic sack of oranges to his chest, and pretended to glance innocently about at his surroundings.

"He's slow, is he?" The woman lowered her voice to a grating whisper.

"Slow?" Jennifer looked up into Dan's face, which was a classic study in self-control. "Well . . ."

The woman appraised Dan once more, without emotion, expelling a small snort of what might have been sympathy for Jennifer. "I expect he's a handful, big boy like that." And with that sage pronouncement, she walked away.

It was Jennifer who finally broke the silence, dredging up every shred of self-control at her command in an effort to sound reasonably serious. "Well, Daniel, what else would you like besides oranges?"

"How long have you been standing there, Jennifer?" he asked in a deceptively mild voice, holding out the plastic sack to her as though it might be contaminated.

She meekly took the bag. "How long? Oh—well, you see, Dan, I had to look for a parking place. I was hurrying—I know how much you hate being alone in the supermarket—when I saw this elderly lady trying to juggle her cane and her umbrella in the parking lot. She had dropped her sack, and her groceries were spilling out in a puddle. I had to help her, of course, I couldn't just leave her there like that. I thought you'd be all right, since Sunny was with you."

"That's very good, kid. Very good," he said in a nasty tone of voice. "Go on. I can't *wait* to hear the rest of this."

"Daniel, it's *true*, honestly, I'm telling you—"

"How *long*, Jennifer?"

She took a deep breath, prepared for his wrath which, she had to admit, was well-deserved. "I don't think I missed too much, actually." She bit her bottom lip and waited expectantly. "Are you angry with me?"

"Angry?" he repeated smoothly, flinging an arm around her shoulder and giving her a rather rough hug. "Oh, I don't get angry, Jennifer—"

"I just get even," she echoed in unison with him.

"You're doin' better, though," he said fondly.

"What?"

"Well, I was expecting you to tear into that poor little old lady with your standard five-dollar lecture on how to treat the handicapped." He smiled tolerantly. "I think it's actually a healthy sign that you were able to stand there and enjoy my misery, Jennifer."

He laughed at her small, disgruntled sound of self-defense. "C'mon, kid. I'll show you how to handpick the finest apples in the county."

Before they left the mall, Jennifer coaxed Dan into a quick visit to the pet shop. He did everything he could to talk her into taking home a cross-eyed Siamese kitten that stole her heart as soon as she walked up to its cage, but she reluctantly left it there.

"I don't know if I can have pets or not. It didn't even occur to me to ask when I rented the house." She glanced behind her as they went out the door.

"Feel free to ask. I've known Joe Como for years, and I can tell you he'd let you stock your own ark if it made you happy."

Once inside the car, Jennifer stared out at the dismal afternoon and the cold rain still falling steadily. "Another few hours of this, and the idea may have real merit."

It was only a little after three, but the slate gray sky and its resulting downpour made it look more like evening. Jennifer drove with the headlights on dim and the windshield wipers on high.

Dan contentedly helped himself to a half-pound bag of M & Ms. "Want some?"

Jennifer glanced at the candy with longing. "They make me hyper," she said ruefully, scooping out a handful.

"What doesn't?"

Ignoring him, she turned off the main highway onto the two lane county road that was a shortcut from the mall to the radio station. "I don't know . . . maybe I should have stayed on the Drive. Visibility is zilch, and I hate this road."

"It's getting colder, too." Dan said. "Better watch the bridge—it might be slick."

Jennifer glanced in the rearview mirror. There wasn't

another car in sight. "Looks like everyone else had sense enough to stay home today."

They lapsed into silence for the next few moments, listening to the station and eating M & Ms. The new disc jockey was doing part of Jennifer's show in her absence.

"He's not as good as you are, you know," Dan finally said, breaking the quiet.

"Why, Daniel—and I thought you hadn't noticed." Jennifer attempted to cover the warm rush of pleasure she felt at his compliment.

"Mm. I notice more than you think. Our advertising's increased quite a bit for that afternoon drivetime. Started about a week after you took the show."

"Aha! *That's* why you noticed. Money talks."

He shrugged. "You're good. You've got a lot of class on the air. You're easy on the ears, witty—" He paused, then added, "Your voice . . . grabs people. Holds them. I think they hear the same thing in it I do."

"What?" asked Jennifer, a puzzled note in her voice.

"The smile in your voice," Dan replied simply. "Were you smiling just now?"

"Yes," answered Jennifer slowly. "How did you know?"

"I can hear it. It's one of the many nice things about you. I don't have to see your smile to feel it. And I think our listeners feel it, too."

Somewhat flustered, Jennifer tried to pass the moment off lightly. She looked at him out of the corner of her eye. "Your shopping is done, so that's not your game. What're you up to, boss?"

Dan closed the candy sack and stashed it between them on the console. "There *is* something I'd like to talk about."

Instantly alert at the rare gravity of his tone, Jennifer nodded her head cynically. "I knew it."

Glancing sideways, she saw him lace his fingers together

and crack his knuckles sharply, an uncommon gesture for him. "Jennifer . . . how would you feel about . . . going out with me?"

"Going out with you?" She parroted his words blankly, her full concentration back on the highway, which was now brushed lightly with a suspicious looking glaze. It was sleeting. Not thinking, she moaned aloud.

"Sorry—it was just an idea." Dan's face went immediately slack.

"What—oh, no! I didn't mean—"

"It's all right," he said quickly. "I don't always read signals too accurately anymore. My mistake."

"*Dan*"—She reached out to touch him quickly on the arm. "I was groaning because it's *sleeting*. The road's horrendous. Not because you asked me out!"

He said nothing. Jennifer looked over at him again, bewildered by the overt tension etched on his face. He looked as if he were about to jump from the car. Daniel? *Insecure?*

Understanding was slow to dawn, but when it did, she responded with customary grace. "You mean a date? You're asking me for a date?"

He hesitated. "In my own inimitable way," he said dryly.

"Oh." It was a small little sound of surprise. Her mouth fell open slightly as she watched his usually unshakable composure continue to slip.

Would she dare?

Why not? A date is only a date, after all. You're with the man most of your waking hours anyway. What would be so different about a date?

An alarm sounded somewhere in her head, warning her that she was already far too attracted to Dan and spent far too much time with him anyway. An honest-to-goodness date would only intensify an already threatening situation, and she really shouldn't. It would definitely not be a smart thing to do.

"Of course, I'll go out with you, Dan," she said softly. "I'd like that very much."

He cracked his knuckles again. "Look, you don't have to say 'yes' just because you work for me. I wouldn't—"

"I didn't."

"Didn't what?"

"Say 'yes' just because I work for you."

"Well, there *are* drawbacks, Jennifer. I'm not exactly your conventional date."

"I don't know that that's necessarily a drawback, Dan," she offered with a small smile.

"You'd have to pick me up, you know."

"That's hardly a problem."

"And Sunny goes with me."

"Sunny and I are pals. What evening did you have in mind?"

"We could ask Gabe and Lyss to come along. That way you wouldn't have to drive—"

"I enjoy driving. When?"

"Look, Jennifer, I want to be sure you understand that—"

"*When*, Daniel?"

He grinned, relaxed his hands, and drew a long breath. "My mother does that."

"Your mother does what?" Jennifer asked impatiently.

"Calls me *Daniel* in that tone of voice when she's irritated with me. How about tomorrow night?"

"It's a week night."

He was instantly wary. "You're busy?"

"Not unless you make me work overtime again, I'm not. Fine. Tomorrow night. But only if I can leave the station by five."

"Four, if you like."

"Deal. Just to satisfy my curiosity, why were you so uptight about asking me for a date?"

"I wasn't uptight. What makes you think I was uptight?"

"Your lips turned blue and you broke the knuckles on both hands."

"I always do that. It doesn't mean I'm uptight."

Jennifer waited.

His expression sobered. "I just wasn't sure you'd want to. The employer-employee thing." He turned his face toward the window on his side. "And the blindness," he added more softly. "There's no waiting list of women who want the complications included in a date with a blind man."

Jennifer remained thoughtfully silent for a long moment. "Well, I think I'm fairly comfortable with most of those . . . complications by now, don't you?" she asked evenly. "Since we're together so much?"

He turned toward her. "Are you? Comfortable with me?"

She had to think about that before she answered him. There were times when she felt distinctly *uncomfortable* with Dan. Unsettled. Even disturbed. But she knew it had nothing to do with his blindness. It had more to do, she suspected uneasily, with some new and unfamiliar emotions that wouldn't seem to give her any peace these days.

She hoped she didn't sound evasive. "I'd say so. I—" She swallowed the rest of her words as she glanced out the side mirror. A pickup truck was moving up rapidly behind them. Too rapidly. She saw him skid on the slippery road once. Then again. But he continued to home in on their tail. Jennifer's hands tensed on the steering wheel.

"What's wrong?" Dan asked, immediately alert to the tension in her.

"I *hate* it when someone does that! There's a pickup truck right on my bumper."

"Maybe if you slow down he'll go around."

Jennifer glanced down at the speedometer and eased up

on the gas pedal. When she looked in the mirror again, the truck had slowed down, too. He was staying right with her.

She slowed even more. So did the truck.

"Is he still tailgating you?"

"Yes. And he's making me extremely nervous. There's ice on the road, and it's not safe—"

"Pull off, why don't you? Let him pass."

"I think I will. He's getting a little too cute." She turned on her right blinker and slowed even more, easing the car over to the shoulder of the road.

By the time Dan heard the sound of the truck's engine, it was too late. It was the same truck, he was certain of it. There was the choppy, distinctive miss of a blown headgasket, the additional loud whirring of something loose or broken under the hood. That was the sound he'd heard the night of Jennifer's party. The sound of the truck that tried to run him down. Or at least attempted to make him *think* he was going to run him down.

"Jennifer, watch out—"

The warning came a second too late. He felt the jolt, the sudden push from the rear on Jennifer's side of the car, heard the loud crunch of metal. He felt her lose control as the car went pitching off the pavement and into a ditch. He snaked out one hand to help her steady the wheel and cried out a sharp warning. "Don't brake! Go with it!"

He heard her ragged breathing, heard her gasp for air, but he could tell by the way she was gripping the wheel she wasn't going to panic. The sudden, careening stop knocked his arm sharply against hers, but they were all right.

He heard the truck go on, heard the sound of the motor gradually fade as it roared on down the road. His hands were shaking as he released his seatbelt and reached for her.

"Jennifer—"

"Oh—Dan, are you all right?"

"I'm fine. You okay, kid?" he asked gruffly gripping her hand.

For a second, they both sat, speechless and stunned. Then Jennifer unlocked her seatbelt and fought for a couple of deep breaths. Without a second thought, Dan ignored the console and moved over the seat toward her, gathering her into his arms.

The numbing realization of what could have happened and the relief of knowing neither of them were hurt abruptly shattered Jennifer's tenuous self-control. She tried to stop shaking, but she couldn't. And when she felt Dan's hands tremble even as he tried to calm her, she started to cry.

He held her for a long time, pressing her face against his shoulder, murmuring soft sounds of comfort against her hair.

"It's okay, now. We're fine, honey, we're just fine."

"But it must be awful for you," she sobbed against his shoulder. "Another car accident after what happened before . . . ."

He shushed her gently, smiling to think that, after what had just happened, her primary concern was for him. He cradled her even more securely against his chest, rocking her back and forth as he would have a child.

"I'm perfectly fine. Gabe has given me a couple of much bigger scares than that in his T-Bird. Don't even think about it."

"But, Dan, that was *deliberate*! That truck intentionally rammed into us!" She drew her head back to look up into his face.

"Are you sure, Jennifer?" But he knew the answer to his own question. *He could have really hurt someone this time,* he thought. A cold trickle of fear iced the back of his neck. *He could have hurt Jennifer.* What was he going to do about this nut? He couldn't just let it go on.

"I'm sure."

"Did you get a good look at the truck? License number, anything?"

"No," she shook her head. "It was a red pickup, that's all I noticed."

He had known it was a pickup, had known by the sound of it the other night when the guy came barreling over the hill at him. But red? He swallowed hard. *Just a weird coincidence, that's all. Don't get strung out over it. Not now.*

He cupped the back of her head and drew her closer again. "Shh . . . there's nothing we can do now. He's gone. We'd better see if we can get back on the road. Are you too shook up to drive?"

Drawing away from him, she sniffed a few times and fished in her jacket pocket for a tissue. She wiped her eyes, pulled in a long, steadying breath, and peered out the windshield. "No, I'll be all right. But we're in a ditch. I think I can get out, though. It's not that deep."

She was still trembling, still frightened. But she moved away from him and secured her seatbelt again. The engine turned over after only two or three attempts to get it going, and after several minutes of rocking the car from reverse to drive, they were out of the ditch and back on the road.

Their conversation the rest of the way back into town was subdued. And Jennifer couldn't stop herself from glancing into the rearview mirror every few seconds. Just to be sure.

6

During the next few days Jennifer found herself growing more and more concerned about Dan's uncommon quietness. He was thoughtful, terribly serious—even moody, she thought. Two or three times she had walked into his office and found him sitting at his desk, raking his hands down either side of his face in a tired, drained gesture, and frowning as if he were worried about something. When she tried to get him to talk about it, he had pretended he didn't know what she meant and quickly changed the subject.

They hadn't gone out again since last week. The only times Jennifer had seen him had been at the station or on a work related project. Objectively she knew that shouldn't concern her. Two dates on two consecutive nights didn't necessarily mean a pattern had been set. Still, she couldn't help but wonder why he had suddenly become so distant.

Today had been no different. They had been on the church bus for over half an hour on their way to a youth rally in Clarksburg and he had said no more than two or three sentences. She had helped him enough at rehearsals with the ensemble to know he was usually buoyant and full of fun when he was with the teens. At the moment, however, he was noticeably distracted and listless.

She decided to make another attempt at conversation.

"Does Gabe always drive the bus?"

For a moment, she thought Dan hadn't heard her. But he finally answered.

"Most of the time."

Something about his hands caught her attention and she studied them. They were clenched tightly in his lap, and he was rubbing them together as though they ached. Her gaze moved back to his face.

"Jason is having a great time up there with Jim Arbegunst and the other fellows. Do you usually bring him with you to these rallies?"

He nodded. "When we can. He likes being with the teens. They give him a lot of attention."

"The ensemble is providing all the music tonight?"

"Mm-hm."

Another long interval of silence followed. Jennifer glanced across the aisle to the other window, staring out with no real interest at the rugged, mountainous landscape. It had turned cold again, and the contoured hillsides were snow covered against a deep gray winter's sky, casting an horizon line so clear it looked painted.

"I think it's going to snow again."

Dan made no reply. Finally Jennifer decided she'd had enough of it. "Are you upset about something?" she demanded bluntly.

That seemed to get his attention. He relaxed his hands as though he had only then noticed what he was doing and turned his face toward her. He looked surprised.

"Upset?"

"You're awfully quiet. You have been all week. Is something wrong?"

He frowned and shook his head. "No. I'm sorry, I guess I've just had a lot on my mind."

"You're sure you're not angry with me or something?"

His look of surprise returned. "Why would I be angry with you?"

"I don't know." She thought for a moment. "I did bug you about calling the police last week, after that truck ran us off the road. I still don't understand why you wouldn't report it."

"I told you why. It wouldn't have done any good."

He knew he sounded impatient and immediately regretted

74

it. He softened his voice and added, "We didn't have a license number or anything. And there are a lot of red pickup trucks in this county."

"Well, I still think we should have told the police."

He could hear the slight edge of resentment in her voice and knew she didn't understand. Why should she? More to the point, how *could* she?

He wasn't sure he understood himself. Much of what was happening in his life made no sense. He was beginning to feel like a marked man. Ever since the incident with the truck last week, the phone calls had been coming more frequently, almost regularly. And Dan had had the peculiar sensation that the caller was angrier and more disturbed than ever. Worse still, he'd had the distinct feeling at least twice this week, late at night, that someone was watching the house. He had tried to tell himself he was just going through another period of anxiety attacks. But he wondered.

The man called the house every night, sometimes two or three times. Sometimes he talked, sometimes he didn't. More recently he'd begun calling the station almost daily. But he never gave any real indication of what he wanted. Over and over again, Dan had asked himself whether the man genuinely intended to harm him or was simply trying to frighten him.

He also wondered if there was any significance to the fact that, as the radiothon drew nearer, the harassment seemed to be intensifying. Any connection seemed unlikely; yet he was beginning to suspect there was one. Could the whole idea of the radiothon possibly be so offensive that someone would go to this length to stop it? It was hard to believe, harder still to understand. Yet he couldn't shake the feeling that in some way the radiothon might well be at the heart of all this.

If he were right, he was going to have to tell someone soon, no matter how distasteful he found the idea. Too many people were involved in the radiothon. He couldn't let his own stubborn propensity for independence overshadow common sense. If he waited too long and this turned out to be more than a scare tactic, he might well put someone else in jeopardy. *Like Jennifer.* The thought stabbed him in the heart.

He reached over and covered her hand with his. "I'm sorry. I guess I *have* been preoccupied," he said softly, turning toward her. "You have to understand. There's this lady in my life who's messin' up my head. I seem to have a lot of trouble thinking of anything else but her these days."

Jennifer studied his face skeptically. "It's all right. I know you're busy."

He squeezed her hand. "Am I forgiven?"

She thought ruefully she could probably forgive this man almost anything. Just as quickly she decided it might not do for him to know that. She squeezed his hand and offered no comment.

Jennifer started through the entrance of the host church with Dan while Jim took Sunny for a pit stop. Distracted for an instant when Gabe yelled a question from the bus, she turned back to Dan only to see him narrowly miss being hit in the face by the swinging church door.

She started to cry out a warning, but it died on her lips when she saw him pivot swiftly away from the door, narrowly avoiding its impact.

"How did you do that?"

"Do what?" He waited for her to guide him down the hall to the auditorium. "I wish Jim would hurry up with Sunny. I could use her for awhile."

"I've seen you do it before," she told him, bending over to pick up some music she'd dropped. She linked her free hand under his arm and began to walk with him. "Sometimes you avoid a collision as if you could see it coming."

"I have facial vision," he replied.

Jim and the retriever came through the door just then, and Jennifer waited while Dan put Sunny's harness on.

"What's facial vision?"

"Radar," Dan said shortly, allowing Sunny to lead him up the steps to the platform.

Jennifer stared at him for a moment then followed. "Figures," she muttered dryly. "Batman and Robin together again."

"Great team," he answered cheerfully. "Jim, if you're going back to the bus, tell Gabe I need him in here as soon as possible to help set up the sound."

"It really is a kind of radar," he went on to explain to Jennifer. "Bats have it. When you move, you send out sound waves that rebound from an object to you. If you really work at it, you can get to the point where you can make a quick estimate of the size of an object. It's helped me save my head a number of times."

He took off his parka, trading it for a contemporary white jacket with push-up sleeves and the bright blue monogram of the teen ensemble. "Give me the layout of the platform, would you? I haven't been here for over a year. I don't especially want to provide any unexpected entertainment for all these teenagers by falling over something."

"You're at the front right now." Jennifer glanced around them. "There's nothing up here except a grand piano and a console organ a few feet to your left. And there's a podium at the far left front. Of course, we haven't got any of our stuff in place yet." She opened his music case and searched until she found the program for the evening, which she'd just that morning typed into Braille for him.

Jason came bounding up the steps just then, screeching to a sudden halt in front of Dan. He started to pet Sunny, then stopped.

"Dan, can I take Sunny off her harness and keep her with me?"

"No. Remember what I told you about that, Jason," Dan said firmly, squatting down on one knee by the retriever. "Sunny has a job to do, and she expects to take her orders from me. When the harness is on, that means she's working and can't play. When I take it off, she knows it's all right to have fun."

"Oh, yeah . . . I forgot. You're her boss."

"Something like that." Dan stood, hooking his thumb in the harness to dangle it loosely over his shoulder.

"And you're Jennifer's boss, too." The frown that ridged Jason's forehead was puzzled. "How does *she* know when it's all right to have fun?"

Dan lifted one dark eyebrow with surprised amusement. "Ah . . . right. Well, you see, Jason, Jennifer likes her work so much she's always having fun." He turned around with a smug grin. "Isn't that right, Jennifer?"

Jennifer crossed her arms over her green ski jacket and weighed her answer carefully. "That's exactly right, Jason," she declared slowly, watching Dan incline his head in anticipation. "That's why I work so much overtime. The fun's the thing."

"*Dan*—" Jason shifted impatiently from one foot to the other.

"All right, all right. Take Sunny and go." Dan hustled him off with both hands. "But stay close to Jim."

The boy hesitated. "Will you be okay, Dan? Without Sunny?"

"I'll be just fine, sport," Dan said with a smile. "Jennifer will be my eyes for now."

He turned slightly, raising his chin in the alert, listening expression he often wore as Jason and the retriever took off. "So—what do you think of my little buddy?"

"Oh, he's adorable! It's just too bad . . . . "

His smile faded. "Too bad?"

"You know—that he's the way he is." Jennifer glanced up

78

at Dan quickly, hearing the shift in his voice from warmth to wariness.

"Retarded, you mean?"

"Well . . . yes."

He didn't say anything for a moment. Jennifer wondered at the somber expression on his face. "Dan? Did I say something wrong?"

"No. Not really." His smile was strained and quickly gone. "I'll be honest with you. That phrase—*it's too bad*—has been a pet peeve of mine ever since the accident. I understand it bothers a lot of people with handicaps. It's . . . a little like someone raking long fingernails across a blackboard, you know?"

She saw him clench and unclench his right hand. "A quadriplegic I met through Friend-to-Friend told me it always made him think of a bunch of mourners standing over his coffin, staring down at him and clucking their tongues over the body."

Embarrassed, Jennifer bit her lower lip nervously. "I'm so sorry. I didn't know."

His mouth softened to a more natural smile. "You couldn't. Don't worry about it. Sometimes I overreact. But what you said about Jason—" He hesitated, took a deep breath, then exhaled it slowly.

"Dan, I didn't mean to—"

He dismissed her protest with a wave of his hand. "I know what you meant. But I don't agree with you. I guess I don't think about Jason as being—different. Just special."

"Are you saying it doesn't bother you that Jason is so . . . *limited?*" she asked incredulously.

He shrugged and scuffed his toe on a raised piece of metal. "You tell me, Jennifer. Is Jason really so much worse off than other kids? Than *normal* kids?"

"But he's such a beautiful little boy!" she countered sharply. "Doesn't it make you angry, Daniel, seeing the unfairness of his life? Doesn't it hurt you, knowing he's—trapped like that?"

"Trapped?" Something flickered in his eyes, the eyes that usually held only tenderness or laughter or concern, and his chin lifted just a fraction.

"Well," she stammered uncertainly, "he's never going to be able to lead a normal life."

His jaw tensed even more. "You see Jason as a tragedy, don't you?"

"I—no! That's not what I meant, I—"

"No? What, then?"

She heard the accusation in his voice, saw the skeptical lines tighten around his eyes. The conversation had suddenly gone out of control, and she felt a distinct need to end it.

"I find it difficult to deal with the unfairness, that's all," she muttered. "I don't understand why God allows some of the things He allows—"

Dan moved just a step closer to her and straightened his shoulders. Then, unexpectedly, his expression began to gentle and his mouth curved into a thoughtful smile. "And you'd like to correct a few of His mistakes, wouldn't you, rebel?" he asked quietly.

"What?"

"Let's forget it," he suggested abruptly, still smiling.

"Not until you explain that last remark." She dug in, not about to budge.

He remained silent for a moment. Then a familiar glint of amusement crossed his face. "You're a contemporary crusader, kid," he said mildly. "In the right country, at the right time, you'd have been a sensational revolutionary."

Tentatively, he reached out to touch her hair, entwining a strand of it around his finger. "If you'd been a little older in the sixties, you would have spent most of your time at sit-ins and protest marches, I'll bet." With a small nod of his head, he added, "Instead, you've ended up with an exasperating blind man and a retarded little boy. No real challenge for a gal with a burning heart."

"At least you didn't say *bleeding* heart," she muttered grudgingly.

"Now you're angry with me." Suddenly he looked extremely vulnerable.

"No." She found it next to impossible to get genuinely angry with Dan, even though he *could* be the most frustrating man at times. But for now, she could feel her petulance fading as she studied him.

His face was so . . . *endearing*, she thought. It was the face of a man who had known great pain and enormous loss, yet had miraculously retained the ability to laugh deeply and live—even love—fully. Shadows had marched across that face, but they had been powerless to destroy the light of the man. A quiet flame glowed from within, the subtle blending of gentleness and strength, humor and kindness and faith that made him Daniel Kaine.

"Jennifer," his soft voice jolted her back to attention. "I wasn't criticizing you." He spread his hands with apology. "We just look at things differently. You see Jason as trapped; I don't. If I did, I'd have to see myself the same way—and I don't dare," he added to himself in a nearly inaudible voice.

"That boy," he continued quietly, "has a precious gift of wonder. He appreciates all the little ordinary things that other people never even notice. To Jason, a colored rock is a special gift. A seashell is magic. A butterfly is a friend. And life is . . . pure, unqualified joy."

The warmth in his tone deepened, and there was real tenderness now in his smile. "He has a faith that you and I can only envy. He *knows* his Father. He holds His hand, he talks to Him about everything that's important in his life— frogs and rainbows and ladybugs, the dream he had last night, the scrape on his knee, the hurt in his heart." He shook his head in a fond, knowing gesture of affection.

"I believe that Jason says 'I love you' to the Lord with every breath he takes. He has an enormous capacity—and a tremendous need—for love. Just like all of us," he added softly.

Jennifer lowered her eyes to stare at the smooth wood floor, feeling terribly young and insensitive.

"Do you really think," he asked with quiet emphasis, "that's what it's like to be trapped?"

"I'm sorry, Dan," she said, her voice breaking. "Obviously, I don't know what I'm talking about."

"You *are* upset with me. Don't be," he said softly. "I hate it when your voice loses its smile."

She turned away from him, feeling a sudden need to hide her agitation, even though she knew he couldn't see her face. "No. Really, I'm not!" she protested, attempting to force a note of brightness into her words.

He stood unmoving, patiently, silently, as though he were attempting to search her mind, to probe the corners of her heart. Neither of them spoke for a long time.

Suddenly, she felt his hands on her shoulders, a light, uncertain touch. Then he turned her around to face him. Looking up into his face, she caught her breath. Something in his expression made her throat burn and swell with a tormented sweetness.

"Jennifer," he said very quietly, his hands tightening on her shoulders, "I wish there were some way I could convince you to let go of your anger."

"Anger?" She looked away from him, unable to endure the depth of understanding and caring that had settled over his features.

He nodded sadly. "Anger. That's what it is, you know. You're angry with God. About your singing career. My blindness. Jason. So many things.

"You think He's unfair. So you beat your fists against His will." His face was tender yet intractable, his voice firm and compelling but not censuring. "It doesn't work, Jennifer. I can tell you from experience that it doesn't work." He brushed her cheek lightly with one finger. "God's not your enemy, Jennifer."

She tensed under his hands. She didn't want to argue with him. She didn't want to explain herself or try to defend herself. He was right about the anger. But she didn't want him to know the extent of that anger. She didn't want to expose the bleakness of her spirit, the weakness of her faith, to a man whose faith seemed to scale mountains and soar with the eagles.

Ridiculously, she almost wished him less than he was, a weaker man, because suddenly she wanted desperately to be big enough for him, to be good enough for him.

Any woman who would love this man, she thought almost sadly, *would have to have wings on her faith, wings that would enable her to rise above the shadows and fly beyond the darkness.* Jennifer knew the wings of her faith were pitifully weak. Perhaps even broken.

When they left the auditorium three hours later, they were met by an angry blast of wind and swirling snow. Obviously, the snow had been falling for some time; the ground was already covered.

"I simply love this weather," Jennifer muttered.

"Did you say something, kid?" Dan put his arm around her shoulder, holding Sunny's harness with the other hand.

She wrinkled her nose and squinted her eyes against the pelting snow. Ahead of them, Gabe was hustling everyone onto the bus, growling out orders to rush the loading of equipment. The teenagers, trying to meet his demands, were running back and forth from the bus to the auditorium, sliding and skating on the pavement as they tugged their instruments up the steps of the bus.

Brushing snow from her hair and her face, Jennifer followed Dan and Sunny down the aisle, exchanging wisecracks with the teens who were already on board. She stopped long enough to settle Jason in a seat beside Jim, then went on to the rear of the bus to sit with Dan.

He waited until she scooted in by the window, then coiled his long frame into the seat beside her, with Sunny settling herself in the aisle by his side.

"This may be a long ride," he said, opening the cover of his Braille watch and touching its face. "We'll be lucky to get home by one if the roads are as bad as Gabe thinks they're going to be."

The words were no more out of his mouth than Gabe stood up from the driver's seat and turned to face his passengers, giving the zipper of his red parka a sharp tug to undo it. His voice was unusually serious and authoritative.

"People, I want you to do your driver a big favor. I want you to just lean back, relax—and sack out! Beginning now. This is *not* a good night for giving old Gabe a hard time. In fact, I strongly recommend that you don't even breathe too heavy."

"Uh-oh," panned one of the boys a few rows in front of Dan and Jennifer, grinning at his seat partner. "Do you think he's trying to snow us?"

A chorus of groans met this remark as the bus started. Most of the teens, already drowsy from the late hour and the rich food they'd eaten at the rally, fell asleep within minutes.

Lulled by the warmth from the heater and the monotonous dull roar of the tires on the snow-covered road, Jennifer felt her own eyes growing heavy in spite of her efforts to maintain a conversation with Dan.

"You look tired, Daniel."

"I am." With a large, contented yawn, he leaned his head back against the seat, turning his face to Jennifer. "You tired, kid?" He reached for her, wrapping her slender hand snugly inside the warmth of his larger one.

"Because my speech is slurred and my eyes won't focus? Nah. Comatose, maybe, not tired."

He laughed softly. "I'll loan you a shoulder if you want to take a nap."

"Mm . . . you're tempting me, Daniel, you really are." Her voice thickened as she fought to keep her eyes open.

"My pleasure," he assured her in a whisper, his free hand gently coaxing her head onto the broad warmth of his shoulder.

"I probably can't sleep, you know," Jennifer protested with a huge yawn, trying hard to ignore the crazy flip-flop of her heart. She glanced uneasily over her shoulder at the ice-dusted window beside her. A fury of snow was pelting the bus, driven by a moaning, angry wind.

Shivering, she nestled a little closer to Dan's warm strength. "Bad weather always makes me nervous."

"Anything you can't improve on makes you nervous, rebel." Jennifer heard the smile in his voice but her eyes were closed now. "Go to sleep. The Lord can handle this one without your help."

Too tired to protest, Jennifer yawned again. "Mm-hmm . . . I s'pose . . . ."

He smiled with enormous pleasure in the dark shadows of the bus, leaning closer to accommodate her head and suddenly feeling like a king when she cuddled contentedly against him. The soft fragrance of her heavy hair drifted up to him, making him slightly dizzy, and he rested his chin on top of her head. *This is most likely the only time you're not actively protesting something, sweetheart . . . when you're asleep.*

When she unknowingly moved her hand, bringing it to lie

against his chest as she steadied herself in her sleep, he gently covered it with his own, curving her fingers under his as though he were sheltering a small dove beneath his palm.

Please, Lord, let it be her ... after all these years of waiting, being afraid to hope and being afraid not to ... please, let her be the one. Within a few moments, Dan's eyes closed, too.

Waking slowly to the tedious engine drone that had soothed her to sleep, Jennifer looked up at Dan from under heavy-lidded eyes. Her heartbeat quickened when she saw the tender way he had locked her hand in his, and a warm blanket of sweetness enfolded her as she gazed up into his sleeping face. His head was nestled deeply against the seat, and his silken charcoal hair was ruffled from sleep, now falling away from his face instead of forward as it usually did.

In the rare vulnerability of the moment, she thought she could detect just a glimpse of the boy he had once been. A soft finger of sadness touched her heart as she studied him, wondering what it was like for him when he woke up morning after morning to the same gray void, as he described it, always the same, whether he was awake or asleep. How did he face day after day of getting up in the dark ... of going to bed with no moonlight creeping through his window, no stars to wish on? How did he live, knowing it would never again be daylight for him?

Such a good, kind man, Lord, she thought sadly, unaware for a moment that she was praying. *How could you let this happen to him? Of all the cruel, wicked people in this world—people who bring nothing but misery to others— why would you afflict a man like Daniel Kaine in such a way?*

A familiar well of bitterness bubbled up in her again, and

86

her thoughts turned even more resentful. *Why Daniel . . . or Loren . . . or my mother . . . or little Jason? Not one of them ever did a mean thing in their lives.*

A random thought of her own personal hurt insinuated itself among the others. Her dream, her special bright, shining dream. The focus of her life, even of her childhood, had been to sing, to bring people to their feet in awe of the music, the glorious, wonderful music . . . .

I won't think about it. I promised myself I'd never think about it.

She looked up at Dan again. Odd, how in such a short time she'd come to count on this man, to trust him and believe in him when she couldn't seem to believe in much of anything else. She thought she could literally throw her life into his hands with complete confidence. What a strange, inexplicable way to feel about—a blind man.

Suddenly, an old, bittersweet memory drifted into her mind, a memory touched with pain and poignant with love. She saw her mother's face, frail and white and drawn in the last remaining days of her life. She heard her soft, wavering voice, once melodious and resonant, now drained of its rich, vibrant strength. And she saw herself, a frightened, miserable, angry teenager, fighting to hold on to her mother. To the end, she had gone on fighting . . . .

It was one of the last times they had prayed together, and Jennifer had had to force herself to keep her head bowed and her thoughts turned to God. She was so terribly angry by then. And afraid. Afraid of what was coming, the suffering her small, loving mother would yet endure, the desperate loneliness her father would have to bear, the adolescent Paul's confusion, and poor little Loren's bewilderment, his total inability to understand, at only eight-years-old, why his irritable, anxious older sister was suddenly doing all the things for him his mommy had once done.

Though weak, her mother's voice had been surprisingly

steady that day, Jennifer remembered.

" . . . Jennifer is such a good girl, Father, a strong girl. She will need a strong man, Lord. I know that even now you are preparing such a man for her, just as you're preparing Jennifer for her future husband. I pray that he will be a very special man, Father . . . very special indeed, for Jennifer is special, too."

She had opened her eyes then and looked directly into Jennifer's gaze, her frail, thin hand clasping her daughter's even tighter. "You must be sure to wait, Jennifer, wait for God's man."

Unhappy, sick with pity and worry for her mother, Jennifer had only managed a disinterested mumble. "Yes, Mother. I will."

Her mother had smiled then, her eyes brimming with love and certainty. "He'll be . . . different, I imagine; no ordinary man. The Lord knows you need a strong, different kind of man to help you harness that independent spirit of yours and bring it into line for God's work." She had moved her hand to Jennifer's cheek, still smiling into her daughter's eyes. "You wait and see, Jennifer. He'll be a very special man . . . . "

Suddenly, Jennifer looked up at Dan and felt a need to touch him. She reached out to smooth a dark wisp of hair away from his forehead. When she did, he slowly opened his eyes and gently squeezed her hand. The warmth of his slow, easy smile enveloped her in its gentleness.

"I didn't mean to wake you," she murmured, thinking she should probably move away from him now, feeling a sudden sense of loss at the very thought.

Had her mind not been so thick with fatigue and clouded with memories, she might have felt a trace of amazement at how easy it was, how right it felt, to be almost in his arms. Indeed, she *was* in his arms, she suddenly realized, with one hand against his chest, still tucked inside his, and his other arm now coming to rest securely around her shoulders. But, groggy as she was, she felt not even the slightest inclination to move away.

"Is it still snowing?" he asked softly.

"Are you admitting a radar failure?" she teased in a whisper. Glancing out the corner of her eye—as much effort as she could bring herself to make at the moment—she shuddered at the nearly total lack of visibility. "It's *awful*! I can't see anything."

He gently cupped her shoulder with his hand, moving her closer to him until her face was almost touching his. "Then don't look," he said softly, smiling the irresistible slow smile she had grown to cherish so very much.

Jennifer swallowed with difficulty, unable to look away from his face. They were so close, their lips almost brushing. But still they didn't touch. She sensed that he was waiting, thinking, wondering, and she felt herself dropping deeper and deeper into the dark stillness wrapped around them.

"Is the gang still asleep?" he finally whispered, moving his hand from her shoulder to lift and comb gently through the tousled waves of her hair with his fingers.

"I think so. Hard to believe so many teenagers can all conk out at once, isn't it?" She felt an irrational compulsion to start babbling, to chatter away the sweet intensity of the moment.

"Mm. No one's awake but us?" His voice was low, so low it made her catch her breath.

"Just . . . us," she answered weakly. Her words stuck in her throat when he began, with an achingly gentle touch that made her heart hammer, to trace the pattern of her face. His rough-textured fingertips traveled over her smooth skin, lingering on her lips. "Why?"

"Because," the word was no more than a whisper as his thumb tenderly rubbed across her dimpled chin, "I don't especially want an audience the first time I kiss you."

She saw his inky long eyelashes flutter uncertainly against

the upper ridge of his cheekbones just before he lowered his head. His hands framed her face as a faint hint of a smile hovered at the outer corners of his eyes. At last he found the sweetness of her lips, touching them with his own in a kiss as light as a tender whisper.

Her heart seemed to melt like a slow-burning candle in a summer night's breeze when he breathed her name, just once, against the softness of her cheek. She could hear his pulse in his voice and her own in her ears, the only sound around them in the darkness.

He gathered her as closely as the seat would allow, kissing her once more, a longer kiss of tenderness and searching and meaning. When he finally put her gently away from him, Jennifer heard him sigh as though it made him very sad.

"Ah, Jennifer," he whispered against her cheek, "you are such a gift ... such a precious gift."

"Daniel—" When she reached up to touch the textured velvet of his bearded cheek, he quickly covered her hand with his own.

"So fine," he murmured, "Everything about you is so ... *fine* ... and you don't even know it. You have no idea how very precious you are ... especially to me."

Her head suddenly began to pound with warning as she tried to fight her way to the top of the drowning pool of her feelings. *It can't be Daniel, Lord ... it can't be him, can it? He's strong—but he's too strong. Far too strong for me. I could never be what he needs, what he deserves, never. I don't understand this man, I don't understand his strength or his obedience to you or his peace. It can't be Daniel ... that wouldn't work at all, Lord ... it just wouldn't work at all.*

She buried her head in the dark warmth of Dan's shoulder, forgetting, for the moment at least, how very different they were from one another and how impossible it would be to ever reconcile those differences.

7

The man leaned back as tightly as possible against the torn seat of the truck. The street light wasn't shining directly on him, but it was shedding enough of a glow to make him nervous.

He worried his lower lip anxiously with his teeth, then sneered at his own skittishness. No one was paying any attention to the truck. Kaine couldn't see anything, and the woman wasn't looking anywhere but at Kaine. The other two, that blabbermouth Denton and Kaine's sister, were looking in the window of the music store next to the restaurant.

Malice narrowed his eyes as he stared at the guide dog walking beside the blind man. He frowned and stroked the deep vertical line that edged one side of his mouth. That dog could be a problem. He might have to take care of the dog first.

He watched the four of them, laughing and horsing around like a bunch of kids as they got into Denton's Thunderbird and pulled away from the curb.

Kaine was all lit up tonight, that stupid grin plastered all over his face. If he wasn't such a Sunday-do-gooder, you'd think he'd lifted a few.

His thin-lipped mouth curled into a contemptuous smile. It was the woman, that's why Kaine was glowing like a Christmas tree. He'd been watching them for over two weeks now. They were almost always together. Sometimes they'd go to her house and eat, then she'd take him up the hill to his place. They went to Como's a lot, too. Sure, Kaine could afford that. He had to be loaded, the way he was always throwing his money around.

Yeah, they were getting real thick. He'd been watching. He

liked to watch her. She almost always closed her drapes over the sheer curtains, but there was enough of a gap at the side of the living room window that he could still see in. When Kaine wasn't there, she'd curl up on the couch with a pencil tucked behind her ear and read or listen to music.

She was a pretty woman, too good looking for a man who couldn't even see her. She had a nice voice, too. Sometimes he listened to her on the radio. But once in a while Kaine would be on the air with her, and then he'd turn them off. He wouldn't listen to them talk to each other on the radio. You could hear her get all smiley when they were together. You could hear in her voice that she liked that big hairy ape.

It didn't matter. Kaine wasn't going to be around much longer. Soon as he tormented him some more, made him pay for worrying him all this time, he'd turn him off for good.

The thought made him snicker out loud. He waited a minute, then pulled out and followed the Thunderbird, staying well behind.

Just as he'd hoped, they went to the Terry woman's house. He slowed down almost to a stop and watched as Denton let Kaine and the woman out, then took off with Kaine's sister.

Good. That meant he'd have time to pay a visit to the blind man's empty house.

He pressed the gas pedal a little harder and took off. He felt anxious and excited. With an ugly sound of elation, he reached into the deep pocket of his hunting jacket. Removing a small flask, he took a quick swig of its contents. After two more gulps he stuck the flask back in his pocket. That was better. He felt warmer now. Ready to deliver his little surprise to the Kaine residence.

He wiped his mouth with the back of one hand, glancing down at the floor on the passenger's side of the truck. A crazed spark of anticipation flared in his eyes as he stared at the gallon bucket and the crowbar lying beside it.

His thin, diabolical laugh bounced around the truck. *You like games, Kaine. You been playin' games with me for a long time, makin' me wait, worrying me half-crazy . . . now I'm gonna have the fun. It's my game now, blind man. And you're gonna be the loser.*

A sudden unpleasant thought sliced through the thick haze of his mind, causing the mad sound of his laughter to die abruptly. *The woman . . . what if Kaine had told the woman?*

Kaine and the woman were always together. All you had to do was watch them and you could see they had something going. Kaine had kept quiet all these years—biding his time, planning to ruin him eventually—but he hadn't had a girlfriend until now. Wouldn't he likely tell his woman?

The slight tremor in his hands turned to an almost violent shake as he fought to keep a grip on the steering wheel. He began to nod his head up and down, pulling his mouth into a furious snarl. *Maybe he already has . . . maybe she already knows.*

He didn't really want to hurt the woman yet. He had plans for her, once Kaine was out of the way. Still, he ought to be finding out if she knew.

He glanced down once more at the floor of the truck just before he turned up the hill to Kaine's place. He decided what he'd do. He'd make his little delivery, then go back down to the woman's house and see what he could find out.

He'd eavesdropped on them before. Standing outside by the living room window, he could hear them pretty good. That's what he'd do. There was time. Plenty of time. This was his game now. He'd call the plays.

He smiled viciously. And he'd name the players. The woman might just have to be a part of the game after all.

8

Dan set his empty pie plate carefully on the lamp table beside the couch. Then he stretched, locked his hands behind his head, and leaned comfortably back against the plump, floral cushion. His face creased with a smile of contentment as he listened to the flames lapping softly in the fireplace.

"Well, kid, your banana cream pie more than makes up for your coffee," he said lazily.

Returning from the kitchen with a second cup of coffee for herself and a second glass of milk for him, Jennifer stopped by the couch and studied him for a moment.

He smiled at her, and she thought with a touch of gentle amusement that Dan always looked much bigger in her living room than anywhere else. Something about the wicker furniture and delicate colors, she supposed.

She put the milk into his hand. "I think you should know, Daniel, that no one else besides you has ever complained about my coffee."

He continued to smile, wisely saying nothing.

"Your mustache is white," she told him dryly as he drained the last sip of milk from his glass. He looked entirely too handsome in that ivory silk shirt, she thought with a mild feeling of irritation.

Sunny stirred restlessly and raised her head looking first at them and then to the window, but as Dan rubbed her head, she settled down again. "Have you noticed how much more relaxed Sunny has been tonight?" Jennifer asked. "I think she's finally getting used to the house. Remember how restless she was last week when you had dinner here?"

"Mm-hm. Well, a lot of things affect her. Even the weather.

She's probably hoping for a reward if she's especially good tonight. Like her own piece of banana cream pie maybe."

"And she just may get it, too. Speaking of *A-wards*, Daniel," she said with exaggerated emphasis, "I read the article in this morning's paper about the one *you're* getting." She sat down beside him. "I can't believe you didn't tell anyone about it before now."

The local paper had carried a front page announcement that a well-known national organization would be presenting their annual humanitarian award to Dan in recognition of his continuing efforts for the handicapped, specifically his work with Helping Hand Farm and the Friend-to-Friend Association.

Obviously unimpressed, he shrugged and set his glass down by his plate, dabbing the milk from his mustache with his napkin.

"You're going to be a folk hero if you get any more awards, Daniel." She was teasing him, but the truth was that he did have a rather impressive variety of awards strewn around his office.

He still said nothing for a few seconds. When he finally spoke, his tone was far more serious than usual. "The real heroes I think, are the ones who don't get any awards." He rolled up the sleeves of his shirt and leaned over to give Sunny, who was now sprawled lazily at his feet, another pat on the head.

"What? Now, Dan, you deserve that award—"

"The ones who really deserve the awards," he interrupted thoughtfully, "are the families and friends of the handicapped. Sometimes it's even tougher on them than it is on us. No one ever thinks too much about what *they* go through."

Jennifer looked at him curiously as she stood and began to collect their dishes.

"When something happens, like what happened to me,

for example, we get so caught up in *surviving*—at least once the initial shock wears off—that we're sometimes too absorbed in ourselves to realize what's going on in the lives of the people who love us."

Jennifer went to the kitchen and began to load their few dishes into the dishwasher, watching him intently across the counter as she worked.

"We get so involved, you know? With the rehabilitation and everything. We tend to lose touch with what our families are going through. To some extent, we can vent our frustration in the process of rebuilding our lives. But the ones who have to stand by us . . . . " His voice drifted off with his thoughts.

Pushing a stray wisp of hair away from his temple, Dan leaned forward and rested his elbows on his knees, lacing his fingers together. "I know my family—and Gabe, too—have kept as much of their own pain away from me as possible." His faint smile was sad. "But they've suffered right along with me. A lot."

"Your family," Jennifer said sincerely, "is nothing short of wonderful."

"They are, aren't they?" he agreed quietly, continuing to smile as he remembered . . . .

His mother . . . the first sound he'd heard, waking up from the nightmare to an even worse reality, had been the sound of her soft weeping across the room. Ah, but once she had realized he was awake, the weeping had stopped. Then there had been only her cool hand brushing his hair away from his forehead as she attempted to communicate what was left of her own strength to him. Even now he could feel her soft, fragrant cheek pressed against his as though she could somehow absorb a part of his pain into herself so his misery would be less.

And his dad . . . kneeling by the hospital bed, gripping Dan's hand as he prayed unceasingly, holding onto him gently, yet firmly. Those skillful, highly trained physician's hands had worked for years to heal the pain and illnesses of others but were now helpless to heal the agony of his only son. Lucas had forced Dan to fight, to reject even the slightest hint of self-pity. He had shed all his tears alone, so his son wouldn't be hurt even more by his father's grief.

Lyss had been there, too, of course. He could still remember lying there, listening to her pace back and forth in her long-legged, smooth, athletic stride. The soft scent of the baby powder she always used had been strangely comforting as it gently touched the hospital room with its familiar freshness. Sweet Lyss, being so strong and cheerful and encouraging . . . and so desperately, quietly frightened.

And Gabe . . . faithful friend and brother of his heart. Gabe, who for years had made the story of David and Jonathan come alive for Dan. It had been Gabe who had held him down with his own body and made him face what he was doing to those who loved him that awful day—or was it night—when he was given the final verdict that destroyed his hope and threatened to destroy his sanity . . . .

"You said you had to know the truth, buddy . . . all right . . . now you know it. And let me tell you, turning into a wild man isn't going to change the truth; it isn't going to make it disappear. You've got your mom one step away from hysteria, and your dad is going down fast. Get yourself together, Dan, and do it now, or so help me, I'm going to punch you out just to shut you up! Your folks can't take anymore, they've had enough—do you understand that, man? No more!"

Dan had reached up to push away his face, to thrust Gabe out of his life along with everyone and everything else . . . and it was then that he'd felt the river of Gabe's tears. He had lowered his hand, wet with the dampness of shared grief, and slowly pulled his friend's head down onto his chest so they could weep together, just as they had when they were children . . . .

Jennifer turned out the light in the kitchen and returned to the couch. "Dan?" Her voice was soft, her touch upon his shoulder hesitant.

It took him a minute to clear his head. "Sorry..." He smiled, and it was a smile deep with a knowing sorrow. "I guess I was thinking about heroes."

She sat down next to him again, and he slipped his arm around her shoulders, an instinctive gesture these days, completely natural, its only intent to keep her close to him.

She leaned back with her head resting on his shoulder, thinking how quickly she'd grown to feel comfortable and secure with this big, gentle man.

"Tell me about your family, Jennifer," he said casually.

And quite naturally, she did. She told him about Paul, now twenty-four, who had a new wife and a new job as a park ranger. "To Paul, there's nothing worse than a city apartment or a crowded room. He would make a wonderful hermit."

Her tone sobered as she told him about Loren, who had just recently turned nineteen. A victim of cerebral palsy, he spent his days in a wheelchair. "He's so special," she said softly. "I don't think Loren has ever been bored, not once. He has this incredible thirst for learning. He'd be—he would have been—a marvelous teacher."

She let her words trail off, then shifted her attention back to Dan. "He and Dad want to meet you. They're both *very* impressed that I'm working for a former Olympic champion."

"Your dad must be a pretty impressive guy himself," Dan commented with a smile. "The last few years couldn't have been easy for him—without your mother."

"Actually," Jennifer answered, tilting her head so she could look up at him, "Dad is a lot like you."

"Oh? And what is a lot like me?" He squeezed her shoulder and gave her a teasing, affectionate grin.

Jennifer studied his face, then replied as truthfully as she could. "He's very strong. Nothing shakes my dad. He simply—copes. He's a rock." She sighed deeply. "He's a people-lover, too—like you. Always finds the best in everyone, never takes time for his own problems because he's too busy helping everybody else with theirs."

She was surprised to see that Dan appeared strangely flustered by her words. His voice was almost gruff. "Thank you, Jennifer."

"For what?" She tipped her head even more with a quizzical stare.

"For comparing me so favorably with a man like that." He turned his face away slightly, but not before Jennifer saw a shadow pass across his features. "I'm afraid," he added quietly, "your observation has a definite faultline in it. But I'm still flattered."

Neither of them spoke for several moments. It was Dan who finally broke the silence. "Your mother died of cancer, you told me?"

"Yes," she replied tightly. "When I was sixteen."

His hand tightened on her shoulder and he rubbed his chin lightly across the top of her head. "That must have been tough for all of you."

When Jennifer said nothing, he asked softly, "Was she ill a long time?"

"Two years."

He nodded with understanding. "You've had a lot of pain in your life already."

Startled, she looked up at him. "Nothing compared to yours."

"Pain is pain, Jennifer," he said, pulling her a little closer to him. "When you lose something precious to you, whether it's a person or a dream or one of your senses, it leaves a hole in your life. And it hurts. Losing something dear to you always hurts."

A hole in her life. That's exactly how she felt sometimes. As if somewhere, deep inside of her spirit, there was an emptiness—a large, dark vacuum.

He pulled her a little closer to him, resting both hands lightly on her shoulders and his chin on top of her head. "Jennifer . . . tell me why you won't sing anymore," he said softly against her hair.

"I can't," she said flatly, without explanation.

"Can't—or won't?" he parried gently.

"Is this a counseling session, Daniel?" Her tone was sharp and guarded.

"Not unless you want it to be," he replied agreeably.

Her short, indrawn breath caused him to brush a light, reassuring kiss across the top of her head. "Let me try to say it for you," he murmured. "It's like . . . an emptiness, a *deadness* inside of you. Like there's nothing where the music used to be except a kind of—silence."

She stiffened at his incredibly accurate perception, then slumped her shoulders under his hands with a small, odd gesture of relief. "Yes," she whispered, not trusting herself to say more.

"I understand that, honey."

She squeezed her eyes tightly shut in response to the endearment. Her heart was aching almost past the point of endurance because she could hear the caring in his voice, the deep, infinitely precious note of tenderness.

"I know that emptiness, Jennifer. I sometimes call it the *vacuum of desolation.* I suppose I could describe in fine detail exactly what you mean. But I can also tell you that it doesn't have to last forever."

His fingers combed slowly and very gently through her heavy hair as he went on talking in a quiet, soothing tone. He seemed to choose his words with much thought and a great deal of care.

"Losing hurts. And so we grieve. There's nothing wrong with that. We *need* to grieve. Grief is a vital part of being healed. It never pays to try to shortcut the process. You have to just . . . go through it, experience it, be engulfed by it. For a time."

His arms around her tightened a little in a protective gesture. "But sooner or later you have to face the pain. You have to admit the fact that you just can't deal with it, not alone. At that point, you have only two real choices. You can accept the circumstance, whatever it is, and lay it down at the feet of the Lord. To do that, you have to believe everything that comes to you first passes through His hand. Even suffering. So by the time it gets to you, you can be sure it's a part of His loving plan for your life."

His voice grew even softer and more serious. "Or, you can fight it. You can throw your spiritual fists up and refuse to surrender. If you choose to fight," he hesitated a fraction of a second, "you leave that hole in your life uncovered, and it just keeps getting bigger. That emptiness will keep on growing until it finally swallows you up, until your entire life is absorbed into that gaping, empty hole . . . and there won't be anything left of you except pain and anger and misery."

"I *have* accepted it," Jennifer murmured dully. "I'm not fighting . . . any of it anymore."

He sighed deeply, gently easing her head to rest in the crook of his elbow as he cupped her chin with his hand and turned her face to his. "No, I don't think so, Jennifer. I think what you've done is *resign* yourself to things. But there's a difference—a critical difference—between resignation and acceptance." He held her tightly but with exquisite tenderness.

"Resignation doesn't leave any room for hope or joy. It's a closed door. And sometimes a lot of anger and resentment are trapped behind that door. Acceptance leaves the door open for God to work His will." He paused for a long moment, then added, "What I hear in your voice, Jennifer, is resignation."

As though anticipating her protest, he stopped her words

by gently touching two fingers to her lips. "Once we grow up, we find resignation much easier than acceptance. When we're children," he said thoughtfully, "joy and wonder and trust just come naturally to us. We accept . . . because we still see God as a loving Father.

"But then we grow up, and we find out about things like cancer and war and famine and deceit. And either we begin to believe that God has changed, and we lose our hope, or we assume He was never what we believed Him to be in the first place—and we lose our trust. As our world gets bigger and wider, we learn more, we see more . . . and a lot of it is ugly and filled with pain. But what we forget is that the God of our childhood is still bigger than the world and all the suffering it can cause us."

He coaxed her head very gently against his chest and simply held her that way for a long time. Jennifer knew in her heart that Dan had just thrown a lifeline to her if she could somehow make herself grab hold of it. She knew the truth and the wisdom of his words. But she thought she could also see something Dan either didn't see or chose to ignore. There were major, significant differences between the two of them. To Jennifer, those differences meant that what was easy for Dan might well be impossible for her.

There was an unbridgeable canyon, she told herself silently, between her and Dan. He was maturity, strength, and wisdom. She was incompleteness, confusion, and rebellion. Unwillingly, regrettably, she feared that no amount of understanding or caring or . . . even love . . . could close the gap between them.

As if he could sense the turmoil going on within her, Dan put her gently away from him for a moment and pulled something out of his shirt pocket. "Here—I brought you something."

Distracted, Jennifer stared at him blankly for a moment.

He pressed an unlabeled cassette tape into her hand. "It's

102

the demo for *Daybreak*. I thought you might want to listen to it. Sorry I don't have a book—all I had at home was my Braille score." He paused a beat and said quietly but pointedly, "You just say the word, and I'll get a book for you."

"Dan, please don't—"

"I want you to listen to the tape," he insisted. "That's all. The music—and the lyrics—are special to me. All I want," he said softly with a smile that made something warm and infinitely tender wrap itself around Jennifer's aching heart, "is to share something that's special to me with *someone* who's . . . also very special to me."

Jennifer took the tape.

Abruptly then Dan stood and pulled Jennifer to her feet. Shifting the mood between them to a more comfortable, familiar lightness, he informed her he was now ready for his second piece of pie. "Before old Gabe shows up and does me out of it."

"Right, boss," Jennifer agreed quickly, grateful to change directions from the serious turn the evening had taken. As the two of them headed for the kitchen with Jennifer leading the way, Sunny stirred, too, and padded along behind them.

"I suppose you want another glass of—"

She stopped dead and froze to a statue as her words spilled into the darkness of the kitchen. Dan crashed solidly into her from behind, and the sudden thrust of his considerable weight nearly knocked her off balance.

"Whoa! Your turn signal's out, lady!" he laughed, clasping her shoulders with both hands, then taking advantage of the unexpected closeness to plant a quick kiss on her cheek. "Did I hurt you?"

At the same time, Sunny uttered a low growl that quickly deepened to a more intense snarl as she charged the rest of the way into the kitchen. She hit the back door full force, barking fiercely and looking back at Dan as though to reassure herself that he was safe.

"What—" Dan instinctively pulled Jennifer a little closer to him. "What's wrong with Sunny?"

"Daniel . . ." Her throat felt like sandpaper, and an icy rope of fear snaked the entire length of her body.

Immediately sensing the change in her, the sudden tension he heard in her voice and felt in her shoulders beneath his hands, Dan tensed, too, and stood unmoving. "What's wrong?"

The skull-like face at the window was gone. He had turned to flee as soon as he'd encountered Jennifer's gaze. But she was still unable to move, riveted in place by the phantom she'd just seen staring in at her.

"Jennifer?" Dan pressed more insistently. "What is it?"

"Daniel," she was finally able to choke out in a hoarse whisper, "someone—someone is out there watching us."

Dan tightened his hold on her shoulders. "What do you mean? Where?" His voice was suddenly rough.

"Outside—at the kitchen door. He was staring in at us. He ran as soon as he saw me."

He heard the tremulous note of fear in her voice, even above the din Sunny was making. Quieting the retriever with an abrupt command, he called her to his side, then stood very still, holding Jennifer firmly as he tried to think.

When Dan felt her slip out of his grasp, he attempted to stop her but she quickly moved away. "I'm just going to look out the side of the window," she whispered to him. "To see if he's still out there."

"Be careful," he cautioned her softly, feeling a swift wave of anger and frustration rising in him at his nearly total helplessness. *Oh, Lord, this is one of the things I hate the most . . . being useless . . . at least help me think straight . . . that's about all I can do . . . .*

"Do you see anything?"

"No, nothing. He probably ran. I think I scared him as

104

much as he scared me," she said shakily.

"What's Sunny doing? Is she still watching the door?"

"No. She's just sitting there looking up at you."

"Then he must be gone. But stay away from the door— and turn out any lights that are on." He hesitated, then added, "If you have any curtains or drapes open, close them."

Dan listened to her moving around in the living room, flipping switches and drawing drapes. The sound he was waiting for came within seconds—the familiar sound of a pickup truck pulling away. His stomach knotted painfully when he once more heard the faint rattle and the recognizable miss as the noise of the motor faded into the night.

When he felt Jennifer return to him and lean against his side, he wrapped a protective arm around her.

"This just infuriates me," she muttered. "I haven't had a peeping tom since I was in college. You'd think—" She stopped and stared up at him. "Dan—what's wrong? You're pale as a ghost!"

Unwittingly, he gathered Jennifer even more tightly against him.

"Dan? What is it?"

He couldn't answer for a moment. His mind was reeling with the significance of what had just happened. *It had to be the same truck . . . the same person . . . .* The realization chilled him. Had he been there to watch *him . . .* or Jennifer?

He was struck by an immense wave of guilt when he realized that his determination to keep the phone calls and threats under wraps might well have endangered Jennifer. If his obsession about his precious independence had jeopardized her in any way, he'd never be able to forgive himself.

"*Daniel—*"

"It's all right—he's gone."

"Yes, I heard the car leave, too, but why—"

"It's not a car, it's a truck."

"Oh—you can tell that just by hearing the engine? That's amazing, I don't know how you—"

"It's the same truck that ran us off the road," he said shortly.

Jennifer stared at him wide-eyed for a moment. "The same truck? Are you sure?"

"I'm sure. You can turn on the lights now. And call Gabe. Then we'll call the police."

"The police?"

He heard the confusion in her voice. "He could come back," he said. "Just . . . call Gabe, would you? I'd like him to be here when the police come. He'll still be at Lyss's apartment. Have him bring her, too. You can go back to her place to spend the night."

"No, I don't need to do that—"

"*Jennifer*—would you just do what I ask!" He felt her tense at the unusual gruffness in his voice, and he added, in a softer tone, "Please. I'll explain more later."

Silently, she moved out of his embrace. He heard her bang into something in the dark, utter a sharp sound of surprise, then pick up the phone.

Gabe and Lyss were no more than three or four minutes ahead of the police, so Dan had no time to prepare them for what they were going to hear. It was Jennifer's reaction he dreaded most of all. He could almost anticipate the way she'd storm and fuss at him.

Within moments, both young officers came back inside from checking the area to report they'd found nothing except some footprints and tire tracks.

"You were right, Miss Terry," said the taller of the two policemen. "He'd been standing close to your front window, and he was also on your back porch. You can track him through the snow."

Jennifer offered coffee to both men, and they drank it in the living room, standing in front of the fire.

It took Dan only moments to fill them in on the harassment he'd been enduring. He stood close to the fireplace and in a calm, quiet manner told them about the phone calls that had been going on for weeks. He described the incident with the truck the night of Jennifer's party, and he touched on his suspicion that someone was occasionally watching his house late at night.

He concluded by telling them what he believed about the man who had been outside Jennifer's house tonight—that he was the driver of the truck that had run them off the road a couple of weeks ago.

For the moment Dan kept to himself his hunch about a possible connection with the upcoming radiothon. Nor did he reveal the depth of anger and the sick hatred he had sensed in his tormentor. Even though he couldn't see their faces, he already knew they were extremely upset with him— all of them.

When he was done, he waited, resigned to the explosion he knew would come, and it did. Lyss was first. She rudely interrupted one of the officers when he started to question Dan for details.

"I can't *believe* you kept quiet about this, Daniel! That was unbelievably *stupid*, do you know that?"

Jennifer quickly sided with Lyss. "Dan, how *could* you? You could have been hurt—or even worse—and none of us would have even known you were in danger!"

Gabe had the grace to wait quietly until the women had vented their outrage before gruffly chiding Dan that he should have at least told *him*. "I have been known, on occasion, to keep my mouth shut if it's absolutely necessary, you know. This wasn't one of your brighter moves, pal."

Knowing it was easier, Dan meekly nodded his agreement

to every charge they hurled at him, making no attempt to defend himself. "If you're all finished, I think the officers have a few questions they want to ask me," he said quietly.

An embarrassed hush fell over the room as the two women looked sheepishly at each other, then at Gabe, who lifted his brows and shrugged tiredly.

"Dan, do you have *any* idea who might be doing this?" asked one of the policemen.

Dan pushed his hands down into his pockets and shook his head. "No, I don't, Rick. It could be anyone." Hesitating, he made a quick decision, then added, "But I've got a hunch this guy may turn out to be someone who's all strung out about the radiothon."

"Why do you think that, sir?" asked the other officer, a rookie Dan hadn't met before tonight.

"Because all the phone calls and everything else started when we first began to advertise the radiothon, when we first started talking about it on the air. And he's made several cracks about me 'minding my own business' or 'nibbin' in where I don't belong'—that kind of thing."

Neither policeman spoke for a few seconds. Finally, the one Dan had called Rick frowned and turned to Jennifer. "Miss Terry? Is there a man who might be upset with you or Dan? An ex-boyfriend, maybe?"

"There's no one like that," Jennifer said firmly. "Besides, I told you I didn't recognize the man I saw."

Again she described the face she'd seen, shuddering at the memory. "I think he was middle-aged—or older. Very thin . . . extremely thin. He looked almost—"

When she stopped, one of the officers gently prompted her. "Yes, ma'am?"

"It sounds ridiculous . . . but he had a face like a—a corpse. Bony, sunken—and very pale." She swallowed against the sour taste of revulsion welling up in her throat at the memory.

The policeman stared at her for a moment, then made a note of her words. When he glanced up, he studied Dan with concern before speaking. "Dan, there's not a whole lot we can do until we can get some kind of lead on this guy. But one thing's for sure—you shouldn't be by yourself until we can find out what's going on. You're entirely too—" He let his sentence drift off, looking awkwardly at Jennifer and Lyss.

"Helpless?" Dan supplied, with a slight lift of his chin.

"Well—not that, but certainly . . . vulnerable."

"He won't be alone," Gabe said flatly.

Dan jerked his head in Gabe's direction, a sharp return obviously on his tongue, but he set his mouth in a hard, tight line and remained silent. It was starting, just as he had known it would.

As the others made ready to leave, he was surprised when Jennifer drew him into the kitchen before leaving with Lyss.

"Dan . . . I want you to know . . . if I sounded angry a few minutes ago, I wasn't. It was only because I was afraid for you. And upset that you've been going through all this alone."

Before he could answer her, she took a quick, shallow breath and rushed on. "What I want to say is that, even though I wish you'd told us, I think I understand why you didn't."

A wave of gratitude, almost painful in its sweet, swift intensity, began to swell deep inside of him, and he fumbled for her hand.

She pressed her hand over his and held onto him. "I think I know what your—freedom, your independence means to you. I also know," her voice sounded small and unsteady now, "that the only reason you finally opened up and told everything is because you were frightened for me. That's going to cost you, isn't it?"

She gave him no time to answer but simply squeezed his hand in understanding. "Please promise me you'll let Gabe stay with you until this is over."

He nodded in resignation. Somehow, just knowing she understood made everything a little easier, a little more bearable. But that shouldn't surprise him. Jennifer had her own special way of making everything she touched just a little bit better . . . at least for him.

9

"Gabe—I want your word you won't say anything about this yet to my folks."

The two of them were sitting at the counter in Dan's kitchen, drinking coffee and talking. It was almost eleven, but Dan was too uptight to sleep, and he could tell by Gabe's voice that his nerves were stretched as tightly as his own.

Gabe uttered a cynical little sound of derision. "You don't really think Lyss is going to keep quiet about this, do you?"

"She will," Dan said meaningfully, "if you ask her to and explain why you agree with me."

"Buddy, you overestimate my control over your sister," Gabe grumbled. "But I'll give it a try. However," he added as if he'd just thought of it, "I'd better call her yet tonight before she has a chance to get on the phone with your mother."

Dan nodded with relief. "While you talk to Lyss, I'm going to do a few laps. I've got to loosen up if I'm going to get any sleep." He stood and walked across the kitchen to the door that opened into the pool area. "Come on in and join me when you get off the phone."

Gabe laced his voice with exaggerated disgust. "You know I believe in total sloth after seven p.m. No, you run along and play, Daniel. I'll talk to the lovely Alyssa and then take Sunny outside for her bedtime thing. Maybe by then you'll have come to your senses."

Dan grinned and shook his head, then went on to the pool.

He automatically flipped on the pool house light in case

Gabe decided to come in after all. He thought he caught a whiff of an unfamiliar odor, frowned, then went on to the small dressing room on the east wall and changed.

He went into the pool quickly, slipping down from the side and plunging himself immediately under the water. He was eager for the quiet comfort, the soothing blanket of calm that would, he knew, soon begin to wash over him.

At first he didn't realize he was in trouble. A slight difference in the rhythm of the water, a barely discernible sluggishness made him suspect a problem with the filtering system. Curious, he surfaced and gasped for air.

The strange, unfamiliar smell he had noticed on entering the pool area now assaulted him full force. At the same time, he felt a thick, sticky mass thread its way down his face and begin to spread over his shoulders. He shook his head violently back and forth in an attempt to throw off whatever it was. When it didn't budge, he treaded water and began to pull the fingers of both hands through his hair and over his beard. The stuff was like liquid glue. He turned a few inches in the water, and when he did, the same viscous muck slapped relentlessly at his upper arms and torso.

For the first time in his life, he panicked in the water. An unholy dread assailed him, and inside his head he could hear a riot of hammering, thudding noises. In desperation he scissored himself and plunged beneath the water, trying to wash away the revolting mucilage strings from his body. But when he broke above the water again, he knew instantly he had done himself no good. The stuff was like tentacles of liquid adhesive, and there seemed to be no shaking it.

He fought to put down the paralyzing grip of panic. Forcing himself to swim, he began to shout wildly for Gabe as he hurtled through the water.

Reaching the side of the pool, he was trying to pull himself out of the water when he heard Gabe's cry of despair. His hands suddenly slipped, causing him to lose his balance.

112

Totally disoriented, he groped wildly for something to hang onto. He cracked his elbow, then hit his head on the wall of the pool before Gabe was finally able to grasp him firmly under the arms and haul him onto the side of the pool.

The room suddenly became a surreal chamber of Gabe's frightened, unbelieving exclamations of concern and Dan's labored, heaving gasps for air.

He felt himself losing consciousness and wondered if he was going to die. Gabe was clutching his shoulders so hard it hurt and lightly slapping at his face. Lights flashed on and off in his head. The smell grew stronger.

Gabe sounded furious, desperate: *"Dan! Dan! Can you hear me? It's all right, buddy, it's all right . . . it's only paint . . . it's red paint, man, that's all . . . just paint."*

Gabe kept yelling at him, crying his name. He was panicky, too. Dan could hear it in his voice.

"I thought it was blood . . . oh, Dan . . . I heard you shout, and I saw you coming up out of that water . . . covered with that red mess—I thought it was blood . . . I thought you were bleeding . . . I thought you were dying, man . . . ."

Dan finally caught a normal breath, slumped in Gabe's arms, and gave up.

Humiliation was no stranger to Dan. In five years as a blind man he had suffered his share of indignities and had survived a number of embarrassing moments. He handled most of them fairly well, and his sense of humor had rescued him more than once from being utterly disgraced.

He knew all this, and therefore he also knew that the way he was feeling right now made absolutely no sense at all. No one but his best friend had witnessed the scene in the swimming pool. But for some peculiar reason he felt like a fool.

He sat on a chair in the large bath in the pool house, docilely allowing Gabe to cleanse him of the red paint. The entire bathroom, especially himself, he thought with a disgusted sniff, reeked of turpentine.

Gabe was doing his best to snap him out of his black mood, alternating his special brand of off-the-wall humor with an occasional angry remark.

"Don't get within ten feet of an open flame for the next few days, buddy. You don't want to be responsible for the big boom all on your own."

When Dan made no reply, he tried a different tack. "Does Jennifer like your beard?"

"What?"

"Your beard, man. Does she like it?"

"How do I know if she—" He thought a moment. "She's never complained about it."

"So you'd like it saved, I suppose."

"Saved?"

Gabe sighed patiently. "It would be easier if it went. Along with an inch or two of your hair, my friend."

Dan made no attempt to match Gabe's humor. His expression was vacant, his voice flat. "I've had a beard ever since the accident. It's just a lot easier than shaving in the dark."

"Right," Gabe said quickly with a sharp look of concern. "Okay. We'll just soak it in turpentine."

Neither of them made any further attempt at conversation for a long time. Finally, unable to stand the silence any longer, Gabe said softly, "You all right, buddy?"

"I'm fine," Dan answered tonelessly. "Just tired."

"The police are coming out again first thing in the morning."

"Why? They weren't able to find anything when they were here tonight."

"It won't hurt to check around again when it's daylight. The guy might have dropped something they missed in the dark."

114

"Did he break the pool house door when he jimmied it?"

"No. The lock is sprung, but the door wasn't even splintered. We'll get a deadbolt put on there tomorrow."

"I'm glad Jennifer went home with Lyss. I'm worried sick that this nut will try to get to her somehow." Dan's face registered the first sign of emotion in more than an hour.

Gabe's impish features turned uncommonly hard and sober. "I still can't believe what he did here. I'm telling you, Dan, we've got to watch you every minute until they catch this guy. He's a real sicko."

"Nobody's going to watch me every minute!" Dan spat furiously. "I had all I could take of that stuff before!"

Startled by his outburst, Gabe halted his ministration to Dan's face and stared at him for a long moment.

"I know," he said quietly with understanding. "But the alternative could be a lot worse. Something you'd better realize. This is no practical joker we're dealing with here. Someone out there," he grated his words slowly with a pronounced emphasis, "wants your skin. Whoever he is, whatever his reasons, he hates you with a passion. We're talking major psycho here."

Dan swallowed hard and slumped a little lower in the chair. "It's Jennifer I'm worried about."

"Well, that balances out, ole buddy," Gabe said lightly. "Because it's *you* Jennifer's worried about. As for me, I'd kinda like to lock both of you up for awhile." He went on tending to Dan's beard, grumbling, "The creep could have at least used a water-based paint."

The dream came again that night. Dan fought it, as always, sensing even in the unfathomable world of his subconscious that to survive it one more time might be one time too many. But it burrowed through the tunnel of his

115

sleep, just as the headlights had cut through the mountains that foggy night . . . .

He felt the car bumping and weaving on the narrow, pot-holed road . . . heard the soft background music of the radio, turned to his own station . . . smelled the unused, leather scent of his new Porsche . . . tasted the dank humidity of the night. He even saw his own faint smile in the rearview mirror as he lightly tapped his fingers on the steering wheel in time to the music.

But this time the nightmare didn't end as it usually did. Even as he awaited the ending with relief, he sensed there was something different about it . . . the dream went on, on past the headlights and the deafening crunch of metal and his scream of terrified denial. A flash of color suddenly zigzagged in front of him, a spray of red and black . . . .

And then it was over, and he was awake. He sat bolt upright in bed, drenched in perspiration and gripped by a new, almost irrational anguish. Without knowing why, he felt more frightened and more terrorized than ever before. Tonight, more than any other time throughout the years, he could have screamed with the need to banish the nightmare from his mind once and for all.

Instead, he faced the sickening, inescapable conviction that it would simply go on and on and on, through countless nights of his life, until he reached whatever waited for him at the end of it.

He was grateful, at least, that he hadn't woke up screaming this time, as he often did, since Gabe was sleeping in the next room. He sighed and kicked the blankets off, then got up and made his way to the bathroom to splash cold water on his face. Sunny padded quietly behind him, waited, then returned to the bedroom with him, as though she, too, sensed the need to watch over him more cautiously than ever.

His head pounded painfully from the dream and his accelerated adrenalin. He figured his blood pressure must approach stroke level every time he had the nightmare, and tonight had been even worse.

For a long time, he sat on the side of the bed and rested his head on his hands, thinking and finally praying . . . .

Oh, Lord, please forgive me for my selfishness of these past weeks . . . staying silent about the phone calls—and everything else—right up to the point of maybe putting Jennifer in danger. It's nothing but pride, and I know it. Help me to get past this willful obsession I have about handling everything on my own . . . just look at where it's taken me now . . . way past common sense, Lord. If Jennifer had been hurt, I think I'd die.

After a while he lay back upon the bed, reached down to give the drowsy Sunny a reassuring pat, and then lay, eyes open, for another hour or more. Occasionally he thought about Jennifer and smiled . . . once he wept . . . and finally he fell into a restless, troubled sleep.

10

Jennifer spent the next few days in an agony of suspense and dread, but the time was ominously uneventful. Even the phone calls to Dan stopped. No more uninvited visitors appeared at her bungalow, no more hair-raising attacks by the red pickup truck took place, and no more terrorizing pranks like the episode in Dan's swimming pool occurred. Unfortunately, no new leads developed in the police investigation either. Dan had had a professional service drain, clean and refill the pool. It had taken most of the week.

By Sunday, she could almost relax and pretend that everything was normal. Almost. But running through her otherwise ordinary daily routine was a web of fear, a thread of foreboding that affected everything she did. Dan had said enough about his own suspicions to trigger a duplicate anxiety in Jennifer, a nagging apprehension that they were fast approaching some kind of flashpoint.

The enthusiasm she had once felt for the radiothon no longer existed. Her initial excitement had turned to fear. Twice she had suggested to Dan that he cancel, or at least postpone, the radiothon. It was wasted breath on her part, just as she'd expected it to be. He met her proposal with a stubborn thrust of his chin and an expression of disbelief that she would even broach the subject.

He was determined to go through with it, and that was that. The best she could hope for was that the police would soon turn up a clue that would lead them to the sick mind behind this entire campaign of terror.

She could still barely bring herself to think about the terrible thing with the swimming pool. Dan finally seemed to be snapping out of the dejection and utter despondency that had settled over him after that awful night. But this entire, unbelievably cruel assault was demanding a toll from him. His step lacked just a trace of confidence these days. His smile faded a little more quickly, and his voice held a note of hesitancy that hadn't been there before. It was as though, Jennifer thought worriedly, small chips of his confidence were being hacked away from him, one piece at a time. She thought it painfully obvious that lately he'd had to work much harder to maintain his sense of humor and his easygoing, imperturbable mindset. But he tried.

As he was trying now. Jennifer held the phone in a slightly exasperated manner.

"*Sledding?* No, Daniel, I am not coming up to go sledding with you and Jason! I am *tired.* Can you say *tired*, Daniel?" Jennifer shifted the telephone receiver to her other ear as she moved the edge of her kitchen curtains back.

An unexpected mid-March snowfall brightened the late afternoon gloom. It *was* beautiful outside . . . but, no. Definitely not. She was going to bed early tonight, just as she'd been promising herself for several days now.

"You may function very well on nothing but adrenalin, Dan, but some of us weaker mortals need a thing called sleep. Today I intend to recharge my batteries."

She could almost believe the apologetic note in his voice was genuine when he answered. "I'm sorry, kid. I *have* kept you moving right along the last few days, haven't I?"

"You might say that," Jennifer agreed dryly.

"Well," he said easily, "I understand. I'll explain to the boys. Jim Arbegunst is here, too, so he can help Jason with his sled. Mom will be disappointed, though. She wanted us to come to dinner afterward. Pork roast and dressing." He paused an instant, then added, "And fudge cake."

Jennifer glanced down woefully at her half-eaten peanut butter and pickle sandwich—her Sunday dinner. "That's entrapment, Daniel."

"It is, isn't it?" he admitted cheerfully.

"Well . . . I'd have to just eat and run. Your mother might be offended." With a frown of distaste, she dropped the remainder of her sandwich into the wastecan by the refrigerator.

"She knows how busy we are," he offered quickly. "She'd probably even send some fudge cake home with you, to save time."

"You think?"

"I'll see to it. You'll come, then?"

"I suppose. But I *am* coming home early Daniel."

"Oh, absolutely."

Suddenly another thought occurred to Jennifer. "What about Gabe? He *is* still staying with you at night, isn't he?"

"Not tonight. He drove over to Clarksburg to cover the concert at that new church that was just dedicated this morning. Remember?"

"*Dan*—you promised you wouldn't stay alone at night until—"

"It's already taken care of, Jennifer," he replied with what was obviously forced patience. "That's why Jim is here. He's staying over tonight."

She heard the displeasure in his voice and was hesitant to suggest that Jim might not be enough protection. "He's only a teenager, Daniel—"

"He is also nearly six feet tall," Dan said very precisely and firmly, "and perfectly capable of providing exactly what I need—a warm body in the house who can see what I can't."

She didn't like it. But he had used his "It's-final-so-don't-mess-with-me" voice. And maybe he was right, after all. The important thing was that he have someone with him who could see.

Not that the man seemed to require a whole lot of assistance, she thought with a slight shake of her head.

Sledding? She didn't even stop to wonder how he'd manage it. *Radar, how else?* she thought with a wry smile, slipping hurriedly into her oldest jeans. She pulled on a pair of leg warmers, then shrugged into an oversized jacquard-patterned sweater, topping it with her hooded green ski jacket.

She was almost out the front door when she decided she'd better take a change of clothes for dinner. Returning to the bedroom, she tossed a pair of ivory wool slacks and a red slouchy pullover into a plastic sack and dashed out the door.

Dan and the boys were already outside when she pulled into the driveway. Jason, out of breath with excitement, met her at the car.

"Are you going to ride on my sled, Jennifer?"

She rumpled his hair and, holding his hand, walked with him up the driveway toward Dan and Jim. "Is that bright red sled yours, Jason?"

"Yeah! Dan gave it to me for Christmas!"

"Well, since red is one of my favorite colors, I'm definitely going to have to ride on your sled."

She walked up to Dan and gave his hand a quick squeeze. "Is it dinner time yet?"

He grinned at her as he zipped up his silver-gray snowmobile jacket. "You have to earn your meal."

She glanced warily from Sunny—who was off her harness and obviously ready for fun—to Jason. "Oh, no," she groaned. "This looks suspiciously like a three-on-a-sled deal to me!"

Dan's arm went around her shoulders companionably. "You catch on fast, kid."

Jennifer turned to Jim. "How do I get myself into these situations?"

The boy turned his haunted, grateful eyes to her, grabbing at her attention as he always did. "Don't worry,

121

Miss Terry. I'll take Jason and Sunny with me."

"You're a brave boy, Jim," Dan said with a chuckle. "And I'm not even going to argue with you." He gave Jennifer a little shove. "All *right*. Let's move, gang!"

"You're really nervy enough to ride on this thing with me, kid?" Dan pulled their sled with one hand and Jennifer clasped his other arm to guide him. Sunny had already run ahead with the boys.

"Only if you promise no belly-whoppin'."

"Well . . . it might be better if you steer," he suggested after a second or two.

"Actually, Daniel, I had already thought of that."

By the time Dan and Jennifer reached the top of the hill, Jim and Jason were already on their first trip down. Jason was squealing with delight and hanging tightly onto Sunny, who was tucked securely between the two boys.

Jennifer almost gave up before they even got started. Trying to fit on a sled in front of Dan was next to impossible. "You need a two-seater," she ranted, eyeing his long legs hopelessly.

Laughing at her grumbling, Dan enfolded her as tightly as possible inside his arms, tucked his legs precariously outside hers, pulled her snugly back against his chest, and yelled, "*Geronimo!*"

Their first slide down was surprisingly smooth. In fact, by their third downhill run, they agreed they made quite a pair and that there was really nothing to it except skill and quick reflexes.

But Dan blew that theory to the wind on their fourth trip down when he accidentally knocked Jennifer's hand off the rudder, causing her to lose control. Before either of them knew what had happened, they found themselves tumbled together in the middle of an enormous snowdrift.

Jennifer scrambled awkwardly to her knees with a dumbfounded, open-mouthed stare on her face.

Laughing so hard he choked on an inhaled spray of snow, Dan rolled onto his side. He caught his breath and quickly molded a sizable snowball, then tossed it with surprising accuracy in Jennifer's direction.

Jennifer crawled toward him, wiping the snow from her face, and began to pummel him with her mittened fists. This only made him dissolve even further into helpless laughter. He finally found the strength to work his way to his knees.

"Don't you beat on *me*, slugger!" he warned, still laughing. "*You're* supposed to be the navigator here, remember? I'm just along for the ride!"

"Ohhh! Just let me up! Get away, Daniel! I mean it, now! Let me up, I'm going to—"

"You're going to *what?*" he drawled, balancing on his knees. "You're all right, aren't you, kid?" he asked with a phony expression of concern. "Here—I've got something for you."

"What?" She narrowed her eyes with suspicion.

"Just open your mouth."

"Daniel Kaine, don't you *dare*—" Her last words were lost in the handful of snow he pressed into her face.

Jennifer then let go with several snowballs of her own, but within a few seconds she gave up. Sensing her surrender, Dan, poised on his knees, smiled a slow, lazy smile, and dipped his head in search of her face. Jennifer obstinately avoided him, deliberately twisting back and forth so he couldn't find her, then breaking up in laughter at the determined smirk on his face.

"Stop that," he ordered sternly, finally catching her chin in his hand and holding her steady. "You're foulin' up my radar." Murmuring a soft, insincere little threat against her cheek, his expression suddenly sobered. He whispered her name slowly, as if he were savoring the sound of it, then covered her mouth very gently with his own.

Something infinitely tender and achingly sweet squeezed Jennifer's heart when he raised his face away from hers after the brief but emotion-filled kiss. She watched him from a soft haze, wondering at the small, choked sigh he uttered as he gently brushed her cheek with a fleeting touch of his gloved fingertips.

Both of them remained silent, unmoving, like two statues in the snow. Jennifer searched Dan's face, then became lost in his smile. Slowly and simply he removed his gloves, tossed them to one side, and framed her face between his hands, holding her gently but firmly for a long instant before he moved his lips to her temple. "Jennifer . . . I love you."

It wasn't only his words, but more the incredible power of emotion behind them that made Jennifer stop breathing. She stared up at his love-softened face, involuntarily reaching out a hand to smooth away his forward-falling hair. Her breath, when she finally found it again, was as ragged and uneven as Dan's.

He slipped his arms around her and gathered her to him, cradling her gently against his chest and rocking her slowly back and forth in the snow. She thought her heart would break and shatter into a thousand pieces when she heard his anguished whisper against her forehead. "Ah, Jennifer . . . Jennifer . . . what I would give to look at you, to see you . . . really *see* you . . . just once."

Those achingly honest, unashamedly agonizing words opened her heart and her senses as nothing else could have. All her fears about being wrong for him, all her doubts about being good for him, were swept away for one wonderful, unforgettable moment.

She pulled her gloves off and cupped his face between her hands, pulling his head gently down to her. "You've seen me more clearly than anyone else ever has, Daniel . . . you've seen my heart," she murmured just before touching her lips to his.

124

His hands trembled on her shoulders, and he made a soft sound of wonder against her cheek. "I know I have the most colossal gall in the world to say this to you." He brushed his lips lightly over the faint pulse at her temple. "And I may be way out of line, but I have to say it now because I might not ever have the courage again."

Jennifer held her breath, half-afraid of what she was about to hear.

He turned her slightly in his arms so he could rest his hands more firmly on her shoulders, keeping her close, yet just enough away from him that she could see his face. Gone now was his expression of uncertainty and the faltering note of doubt in his voice. Instead he wore a look of inevitable decision, the expression of a man who has met his destiny and is about to surrender to it.

"I am head-over-heels, hopelessly in love with you, my sweet rebel." The tenderness that settled over his face caught Jennifer's heart by surprise and held it gently captive. "I think," he continued softly, "I was totaled the first day you walked into the station."

A fleeting streak of insight darted across his face. "You're the missing part of me, love, and I'll never be a whole man without you. Jennifer . . . would you marry me?"

She could say nothing, do nothing but stare at him, as limp beneath his hands as a rag doll. She hadn't expected this. Of course she'd known he cared for her . . . but *love*? *Marriage*? Impossible. She was light years away from this man in every way that mattered.

"I know I can't offer you anything but broken pieces," he was saying quietly, "but I'll love you more than any woman has ever been loved by a man. I can promise you that much, at least."

Jennifer looked at him with real despair in her eyes. Swallowing with extreme difficulty, she cleared her throat, unable to face the growing question settling over Dan's face.

"Dan...I don't know. I'm not sure, that is—what to say...."

His eyes crinkled with a touch of amusement, even though his voice was unsteady. "How about something like, 'I can't live without you, Daniel' for starters? I could be content with that. For awhile, anyway."

"Oh, Dan—I *do* care for you, but—"

"How much?" His hands tightened on her shoulders.

"What?"

"How much do you care for me?"

"Well, I can't put something like that into words, exactly. I can't just—"

"Try."

She gaped at him, her mind suddenly reeling at this whole impossible situation. "Well, a *lot*, I suppose, but—"

"Do you love me, Jennifer?"

"*Daniel*, you don't just answer a question like that in the middle of a snowdrift. Besides—we really haven't known each other long enough to—"

"Do you *love* me, Jennifer?"

He reached for both her hands and enfolded them between his own. With an expression of great patience, he waited.

"Now, Daniel...you know we're nothing alike. In fact, we're total opposites."

He nodded agreeably.

"Oh, we may have a few things in common," she conceded, "but basically we're like—"

"Oil and water," he supplied helpfully.

"Well—that might be a bit extreme. But certainly we don't see things the same at all. You're very patient, and I'm not."

"Mm. That's true."

She looked at him, distrustful of his complacency. "You're very—accepting. And tolerant. And we *both* know I'm not."

He nodded his head sagely. "I'm afraid that's also true."

126

"You don't let anything bother you. You're just a very laidback, easygoing man."

"Granted."

"You're—philosophical. And I'm analytical. You're careful and thorough and organized. I'm impetuous and messy and scatterbrained. And tense. I'm very tense. I'll probably have ulcers by the time I'm thirty."

"Marry me and have kids instead." He raised both her hands to his lips and skimmed a gentle kiss over her knuckles.

"And we never agree on anything, besides—" She glanced up at the lazy smile on his face. "What did you say?"

"I think I just proposed again." He smiled blandly.

The soft touch of amusement in his voice faded to a more serious tone. "Tell me something, Jennifer. Does my blindness have anything to do with the way you're stalling?"

She gasped, horrified that he could think that after all this time. "You *know* better than that!"

Jennifer was certain a subtle look of relief crossed Dan's face before he spoke again. "I had to ask. You, more than anyone else, know the problems that will accompany me into a marriage. If you think we can handle those, then I think we can deal with just about anything else."

"Oh, Daniel," she moaned softly with discouragement, "it couldn't possibly work. You're—a wonderful man. You're sweet, and you're strong—and thoughtful. But you deserve someone who's like you. We both know I'm not."

"Jennifer—my love—" He smiled at the sound of his own words. "I'd do anything I could to burst this illusion you seem to have formed about me."

He held her hands under his chin and smiled gently into her face. "My love," he repeated, "there is nothing special or unusual or unique about me. If I were as strong as you seem to think, I'd get out of your life. No, love, I'm just a man—a very ordinary man who wants the same things most ordinary men want. I may have a little less to offer than some, but I intend to make up for it with even more love and attention. All I want," his voice was little more than a whisper, "is a lady to love, a home, and some kids to call me 'Daddy.' "

Once more he asked her. "Jennifer . . . do you love me?"

She held her breath. She saw his hopeful expression change to a stricken look of defeat. Without quite knowing what she was doing, she moved more closely into his arms. "I'm afraid I do," she replied simply in a voice so faint it was nearly lost in the wind.

She glanced up into his face then, and she thought the look of growing surprise and relief and happiness settling over him was the most beautiful thing she'd ever seen in her life.

He wrapped her snugly in his arms and whispered against the hollow in her cheek. "Don't be afraid, honey. Don't ever be afraid to love me. I'll never hurt you, Jennifer. Don't you know by now that I'd die before I'd ever hurt you?"

They remained silent for a long moment, locked in each other's embrace.

Jennifer finally broke the quiet. "Dan—I *do* love you. But that doesn't mean I'm ready to talk about marriage yet."

"I'm really sorry to hear you say that, Jennifer," he said with mock disapproval, "because if your intentions are anything other than honorable, this relationship will never work."

"Stop that!" she scolded, poking a finger into his chest. "This is very serious, Daniel."

"Uh . . . can I say just one thing, love?"

"What?" she snapped.

"I hear the happy sound of children's laughter. Could we possibly continue this conversation where it's a little warmer and a whole lot more private?"

Startled, Jennifer peered over his shoulder. Sure enough, Jim and Jason and Sunny were barreling over the slope of the hill, only a few feet away from them. "We may be able to manage the warmth by going inside to the fire, Daniel. But privacy? Don't count on it."

Later, after everyone had changed into dry clothes and warmed up with hot cocoa, Dan agreed to let both boys use the pool. "But we have to leave here no later than five if we don't want to miss dinner. So when I say it's time to get out, you guys better move."

Sunny, obviously determined not to miss the fun, squeezed through the door with them when they left the kitchen.

"It's odd how well they get along together, considering the age difference," Jennifer commented. She was sitting on one side of the kitchen counter, noting Dan's easy but precise movements as he placed their cups in the dishwasher and wiped off the sink with a sponge.

"Jim is absolutely starved for attention, for someone to care about him."

Startled, Jennifer asked, "But what about his father?"

Dan released a half-sigh and dried his hands on a towel. "He's such a lonely, unhappy boy. Sometimes," he said with a disturbed frown, "I get the feeling that his father's only idea of attention is a strong rod."

Dan walked around to Jennifer's side of the counter and tugged lightly at a damp strand of hair. "So," he said abruptly, "have you listened to the tape I gave you yet?"

"No, I haven't listened to the tape you gave me yet," she retorted airily. "When exactly do you think I would have had time?"

"I seem to remember you having a cassette deck in your car," he countered dryly. "Why are you putting off listening to it?"

"I'm *not* putting it off."

A knowing smile curved his mouth but he said nothing.

"I really *haven't* had time, Daniel. And we know whose

fault that is."

He shrugged agreeably. "It's just as well, maybe. There's something else I probably should have given you first."

Dan walked to the large rolltop desk that sat between the dining area and the living room, returning with a black, loose-leaf notebook.

"What's this?" Jennifer asked him as he laid the notebook on the counter in front of her.

"It's . . . a kind of journal," he said quietly.

Jennifer glanced curiously from his face to the notebook. "A journal?"

He nodded. "It's something I started not too long after the accident."

He went into the living room and bent down to stir up the fire. Then he straightened and turned back to her, shoving his hands down in his pockets and scuffing his toe idly on the hearth. He stood silently for a moment, and Jennifer could tell from the way he was digging at the hearth with his foot that he was remembering.

His attention abruptly shifted back to her. "I'm sure it'll be hard to read." He laughed lightly. "My handwriting was pretty bad even when I could see. I didn't start typing any of it until later."

He lifted his chin, his face a mixture of thoughtfulness and uncertainty. "I just thought it might help you . . . with some of the questions you seem to have about . . . things," he said cautiously. "I thought—" he choked off a sound of frustration. "I don't know *what* I thought! I'm sorry, Jennifer, I don't have any right to push my thoughts onto you." He turned away from her to face the fireplace.

Jennifer stared at his back a moment, then glanced down to the notebook. She opened it and began to leaf through it, her eyes drawn to his scrawled, uneven writing on the first few dog-eared pages. There seemed to be page after page of Dan's own words, miscellaneous quotes, and Scripture verses.

Something sad and poignantly tender wafted through her as the significance of what she held in her hands finally registered. There before her were months of Dan's most personal, excruciating agony . . . hundreds of his heart-rending, soul-searching thoughts and discoveries. He was opening his deepest, innermost feelings to her.

She got up very slowly and walked to him, her eyes never leaving the back of his head. When she reached his side, she lay her hand gently on his shoulder and waited for him to face her. "Daniel," she said softly, "are you sure you want me to read this?"

He nodded slowly but didn't answer right away. Finally, he said very quietly, "Yes. I do. And not altogether because I hope you'll find something in it to help you. Part of my reasons are selfish, I suppose."

His voice was gentle and steady as he tried to explain. "I think I'm selfish enough to want you to understand what it was like—after the accident—and coward enough not to want to tell you."

She stared up at him, then shook her head slowly from side to side. "No—" Her voice broke and she hesitated, "I don't think so. I don't believe you have a selfish or cowardly bone in your body, Daniel Kaine."

He frowned at her words. "And that's another reason I think you need to read it, Jennifer. Sooner or later, you're going to realize I'm not the man you think I am. We'll both be better off if you know it now, not later."

Saying nothing, Jennifer studied him carefully for a long time. Finally, she dropped her hand from his shoulder and hugged the notebook tightly against her heart. "Will you tell me one thing, Dan? Why are you so determined that I . . . learn to accept things the way you do? Why does it matter to you?"

He didn't respond right away. Reaching for her hand, he moved her toward the couch and pulled her down beside him. He kept her hand tucked securely within his and smiled sadly at her before he spoke. "Jennifer, I love you too much to ignore your hurt, the pain I hear in your voice."

His face softened even more. "With all my heart, I want you to be able to just surrender to the Lord and acknowledge His right to do with you whatever He will."

He drew her closer, as if to transfer his feelings from himself to her. "I just want to help you see that once you stop fighting Him, at that very point you win." Dan held her tenderly but firmly. "Jennifer, He will never, ever give you less than His best for your life. Even when it involves loss or suffering or a broken heart, He knows exactly what He's doing."

She sighed softly and looked at him with regret. "How can I ever accept what I don't understand, Dan?"

He moved her closer, gently coaxing her head onto his shoulder, and began to stroke her hair gently. "That's your problem, love," he said quietly. "You try to understand first. The fact is, though, that understanding isn't important. There will always be things that are beyond our understanding. That's why it's absolutely essential that we accept His wisdom and His love."

He seemed to consider his next words with extreme care and much thought. "We see today . . . but He sees eternity. We want our comforts . . . but He wants our maturity. We strive for happiness . . . but He offers the pain of growth. We live for ourselves . . . but He says 'die to yourself—live for Me.'"

There was silence between them for several moments. Jennifer searched her heart for words to explain herself, but there were none.

"Daniel . . . it isn't that I don't want what you're talking about," she murmured finally against the soft flannel of his shoulder. "I *do* want it. But I don't know how to find it. I've been a Christian most of my life, but I still don't have the kind

132

of faith you're talking about. And I don't know that I ever can."

Slowly and gently he cupped the back of her head with one hand and held her that way as he spoke. "Honey, the faith I have—whatever I have—is only what He gave me when I stopped ramming my head against His will."

He hesitated, then once again seemed to search for just the right words. "Jennifer . . . this may make no sense at all to you, but I can tell you truthfully that I never knew the meaning of peace until after I lost my sight. The Lord used that time to teach me something I might never have learned otherwise. Oddly enough, the key I found is in the book of Scripture I was named after—the book of Daniel.

"Remember when King Nebuchadnezzar warns Shadrach, Meshach and Abednego that, unless they worship the golden image, he's going to toss them into the fire? I'd read that story for years without paying any real attention to their answer. But once I finally realized what they were saying, I knew I'd found a key that would unlock a whole new kind of faith for me. Remember? They told the king that their God *was able to deliver* them out of the fiery furnace, but that *even if He didn't,*' they weren't going to stop worshiping Him and start bowing down to an idol."

She moved in his arms just enough so that she could see his face. A spark of genuine excitement now flickered there. "That's what *I* had to learn. I accepted Christ as my Savior when I was eight. But I had never let Him be *Lord* of my life. I had to realize that He has the right to either deliver me or not deliver me. But I *don't* have the right to base my love and trust for Him on what He does for me."

Something deep within Jennifer began to stir ever so slightly. Dan's words had struck a distant chord, and she caught an almost imperceptible glimpse of a forgotten hope.

She still didn't understand. But she believed him. He was talking about a kind of peace that she knew would change her life. And she wanted it desperately.

Slowly she lifted her head to stare up at him. "Daniel . . . will you pray for me?" she asked him abruptly.

His slow-spreading smile was soft and wonderfully tender. The affection that settled over his features made Jennifer's eyes mist. "Love of my heart," he said in a voice thick and husky with emotion, "I've been praying for you since that first day you crashed into my life. Why would I stop now?"

11

Late Wednesday afternoon, everyone at the station was racing against the clock in an attempt to get caught up before the beginning of the radiothon on Friday. Jennifer and Dan had been swamped all day, trying to clear up last-minute details between their spots on the air, advertising meetings, and eleventh-hour instructions to other members of the staff.

They were just about to finish up the afternoon drivetime. Dan had volunteered to help Jennifer jock her show today so she could move in and out of the studio to work on other projects as necessary.

"I put that cart you wanted Jay to use this evening right on top," Jennifer said as the last record was ending. "And an extra copy of tomorrow's log so he can double check it."

Dan nodded, waited a few seconds, and opened his mike for the last spot of the afternoon.

" . . . Just a quick reminder about the weekend radiothon." He spoke into the microphone in his slow and easy drawl. "Beginning Friday night at eight o'clock, we're going to furnish you with thirty-six straight hours of your favorite Christian music, some guests you won't want to miss, and, of course, our own Jennifer Terry, doing her incomparable imitation of Mighty Minnie Mouth . . . . "

Grinning at himself, he went on digging at Jennifer, taking a few stabs at Gabe, then he turned serious. "On the sober side, people"—Jennifer groaned at his unintended pun—"if you listen to us even thirty minutes a day, you know by now what this weekend is all about. We're after all the phone calls, letters and donations we can muster to put some serious pressure on the people who are making this country's drunk driving laws."

He paused for only an instant, long enough for his voice to turn gravely serious. "Most of you know me, so you know that I'm a victim. A victim of a drunk driver—just one of many. I'm blind because of someone's lack of judgment and total disregard for human life. There are hundreds of thousands of us out here—victims of drivers who got behind the wheel when they shouldn't have. But, friends—I'm one of the *lucky* ones."

Jennifer froze, fascinated by what she was hearing. She'd heard some very straight talk from Dan since he'd begun to spot the radiothon, but not like this. The expression on his face was steady and calm, but she knew him well enough by now to know that he disliked any mention of his handicap over the air. He was always extremely careful not to exploit his blindness. He wouldn't consider a "personal pitch," as he referred to it, unless it was absolutely necessary to benefit someone else.

"I'm more fortunate than several thousand others," he continued, "because I'm *alive*. A lot of victims of drunk drivers don't live to protest. I did. And quite frankly, I don't like what was done to me. The quality of my life isn't what I'd hoped for. I had something very precious taken away from me, and I had absolutely nothing to say about it. But thousands of people every year, many of them not yet old enough to vote, lose something even more precious than I did. They lose their lives. That's what this weekend is all about. I'm asking you to stay with us for those thirty-six hours and listen to some of the things we hope to accomplish with these nationwide radiothons, then do your part to help. Please."

He closed his mike, took off his headset, and walked slowly out of the studio as if he'd just completed a routine broadcast. Jennifer followed him with scalding tears in her eyes and an enormous lump in her throat, so proud of him she could have cried out, yet so angry at what had been done to him she would have lashed out in fury had there been somewhere to strike.

Two hours later, she was still in her office, sorting through programming schedules for the weekend, checking the log, and trying to get as much as possible buttoned down for Gabe. She was bone-tired. She'd planned on being home before five today, but there had simply been too much to do.

Just as he'd promised earlier, Dan was giving her Sunday through Tuesday off after the radiothon. It would be a much-needed break by the time this weekend was done, and she was looking forward to spending it with her dad and Loren in Athens. She hadn't been home for more than one day at a time since she'd moved to Shepherd Valley, and her dad had sounded a little put out with her the last time she had called him.

Finally done, she stacked the file folders neatly on the credenza behind her desk and rose from her chair with a tired sigh, stretching her arms wearily and yawning. She crossed her office and entered Dan's.

"Dan, do you want that guest schedule tonight or can I wait until tomorrow? Oh—sorry, Gabe. I didn't know you guys were busy." She turned to leave, but Gabe, bent over Dan's desk with a sheet of Braille notes, glanced up and gestured for her to stay. "We're done, Jenn. Don't leave."

Dan stood up as Gabe stepped away from his desk. "Go home and rest," he told Jennifer. "You sound exhausted. We can finish up the rest of the schedules tomorrow."

"That was the right answer," Jennifer responded gratefully. "Well, good night, guys," she told them after another huge yawn. "I'm getting out while I can." She started to leave, then turned back. "You're taking Dan home?" she asked Gabe.

He nodded. "After I take him to Sager's for a chili dog."

Dan groaned and made a face. "We got a standby

frequency for medical alert, Jennifer?"

She waved to Gabe and went back to her own office to get her coat. On her way out of the lobby, she noticed a package the size of a shoebox wrapped in brown postal paper sitting on top of the receptionist's desk. Curious, she stopped and picked it up. Seeing that it was addressed to Dan, she tucked it under her arm and walked back down the hall.

"Here's a package for you, Dan. One of the parcel services must have brought it late this afternoon," she said as she entered his office again.

Gabe had gone back to his office, and Dan was bent over, his back to her, fastening Sunny's harness. "Go ahead and open it, will you?"

"Maybe it's the new postal scale I ordered for us," she said, popping the white string around the package and tearing through the paper. "Nope. It's a shoebox."

Dan straightened and walked over to the desk. "I didn't order any shoes. What is it?"

Flopping her purse down on his desk, Jennifer pulled the lid off the box and looked down inside. Her eyes focused on the contents, then grew wide as her mind began to roar and pound with pain. Certain she was wrong, that she couldn't possibly be seeing what she'd at first thought she was seeing, she took hold of the box with both hands and raised it for a better look.

Only then did she scream the first time. And then again. Sunny barked, and Dan lunged and stumbled into the side of the desk before the retriever could block him.

He reached for Jennifer, grating out her name with alarm, as she flung the box onto his desk with a shriek of terrified disgust.

"Jennifer—*what*—"

At the same time, Gabe crashed through the office door. He stopped dead when he saw Jennifer staring down at the desk and Dan groping for her. "What's going on—" He charged toward them, shoving himself between Dan and Jennifer, grabbing Dan's arm and Jennifer's shoulder at the same time.

Jennifer raised her stunned, near-wild eyes to Gabe, then motioned to the box that she had flung onto the desk top. He glanced down into the box, which had landed right side up.

Unwillingly, Jennifer's panicked gaze followed his as her body arched sharply in rebellion. Every thread of reason left to her cried out in denial, but the vision before her was brutally real.

A strange, chilling calm settled over her as she studied the field mice resting in the box. Three of them. They had no eyes. And they were dead. She glanced up and met Gabe's shocked stare. Their eyes locked for several seconds, almost as if they'd forgotten Dan was even in the room, until his harsh whisper cut into their horror.

"Will you please tell me what's wrong? What's in the package?"

Jennifer noted blankly that he was rigid with tension, his knuckles white as he gripped Sunny's harness.

Her gaze met Gabe's again. He was deathly pale. His usually laughing eyes, dark and stormy, darted back and forth from Dan's face to Jennifer's. "Sick—" his voice was uncommonly weak, and the fingers stroking his mustache were trembling. "Really sick."

Dan took a step around the desk and began to move his hand over the top of it, fumbling for the box. Gabe whipped his arm out to stop him. *"Don't!"* he warned hoarsely. "Don't . . . touch it."

Dan slowly pulled his hand back, away from the desk. "Jennifer? What is it?"

She moistened her lips nervously, tried to swallow, but instead choked off a sob. "Oh, Dan . . . it's—"

He waited quietly.

"Field mice. Dead . . . field mice."

"Field mice?" he repeated blankly.

She nodded, then caught herself, "Three ... three of them." She stopped, looking uncertainly at Gabe, who gave a brief, reluctant nod.

"They have—they have no eyes."

She grasped Dan's forearm with her hand, watching him closely.

He had started to move on around the desk but paused when he heard her words. Jennifer saw his hands knot into tight fists, then unclench. He looked stunned. Stunned and extremely vulnerable. "No eyes?" he repeated softly, then nodded with understanding. "Three ... blind ... mice."

Jennifer moved closer to him, and he absently draped his arm around her shoulder. "Kind of a weird way to make a point, isn't it?" His voice was low and none too steady.

Gabe pulled a piece of paper from beneath the dead mice with an expression of distaste. "There's a note," he said, his voice hard and furious. Jennifer could sense his barely controlled rage.

"Read it," Dan said evenly.

Gabe read it to himself first, glanced at Jennifer, then cast a worried look at Dan.

"Read it, Gabe," Dan said again.

A muscle at the side of Gabe's mouth twitched a couple of times as he cleared his throat. "It says—*This is no bluff, blind man.*"

Jennifer saw Gabe's eyes cloud dangerously. She sensed that he was only one short step away from exploding. He held up the note and began to ball his hand into a fist, as though to crumple the paper.

"Gabe—no!" Jennifer cried quickly. "Don't tear it! We have to show it to the police!"

He stopped, looking from her to the note, then pitched it onto the desk. "I'd better call them," he said tightly, his mouth twisting into a fierce scowl.

He moved toward Dan's phone, then stopped, looking from Jennifer to Dan. "This creep is a total lunatic. A psycho. He isn't just out to scare someone. He's going to try to kill you, Dan. Make no mistake about that, man—he's going to try to kill you." He picked up the telephone receiver and hurriedly scanned the front of the phone directory for the number of the police.

Jennifer didn't realize how tightly she was gripping Dan's arm until he gently pried her fingers loose and tucked her hand securely inside his own. "You all right, honey?" he asked softly with concern.

She stared up at him, trying to discern what he was feeling. "I'm frightened," she replied simply.

He squeezed her hand reassuringly. "Don't be scared. It'll be all right. Maybe he's just trying to make us back off from doing the radiothon."

"You know better than that! But maybe we *should* postpone it. At least until—"

He took in a deep sigh. "Jennifer . . . I can't cancel it now. Look at the time and the work and the money we've sunk into this. We *have* to do it. If I let every kook who didn't like my choice of programming dictate what I do or don't do, I'd soon be off the air for good!"

She stared up into his face, at his seemingly composed expression. "How can you *not* be afraid, Daniel? Don't you realize what he's threatening to do?"

He pulled her a little closer and stroked her hair lightly. "Let's not assume anything until we talk to the police, okay? Let's see what they think about all this."

The police thought the threat was real enough and that Daniel should have round-the-clock protection. The problem was that they simply didn't have the manpower to provide it. But they promised to work out some kind of coverage, at least throughout the radiothon.

141

Dan rebelled at the idea, just as Jennifer and Gabe expected he would. But in the end, the firm, commonsense demands of the police stopped his protests. It was decided that Gabe would spend the night at Dan's house with an officer stationed outside.

When one of the policemen stated that a man would also be placed outside Jennifer's house, Dan turned sharply in the direction of the officer's voice. "You think she's in danger?"

The young patrolman hesitated before answering, darting a quick glance at Jennifer. "I think we don't want to take any chances, Mr. Kaine. We don't know what kind of crazy we're dealing with. And someone *was* outside Miss Terry's house the other night."

Jennifer felt a cold stream of fear trickle down her spine, but she was far more concerned about Dan, whose hand had tightened protectively on hers.

"Gabe," she said weakly, "couldn't the two of you stay at Dan's parents—just for tonight?"

"*No.*" Dan's retort was curt and sharp.

Gabe looked at him thoughtfully. "That might not be such a bad idea, Dan—"

"And it's not a good one, either," he responded shortly. "We're not bringing my folks into this mess. It wouldn't do a bit of good, and we're not going to tell them anything about it, Gabe! Forget it."

Gabe rolled his eyes at Jennifer and shrugged. "You're the boss," he said grudgingly. "Okay. Why don't we get out of here so everyone can get some rest?"

It had been years since Jennifer had spent a totally sleepless night. Not since her last week in Rome, after her hopes and dreams had been crushed by the blunt pronouncement of *Maestro Paulo* had she sat in a darkened room and watched the long, tedious hours of the night plod

142

wearily toward dawn.

Tonight seemed even more endless. The presence of the unmarked patrol car gave her no comfort. She could only think of Dan.

Finally, in desperation because she knew she might go mad by morning if she didn't find something to help her pass the hours, she placed the *Daybreak* demo tape in her tape player and lay facedown on the bed to listen to it. She remembered the notebook Dan had given her, but she was too keyed up to read.

An hour later, she played the tape all over again. It was, quite simply, one of the most powerful musical scores she'd ever heard. It was a musical journey, a journey through the darkness of despair—as detailed by the blind man Jesus healed; a journey through the darkness of sin—Mary Magdalene's account; and a journey through the darkness of unbelief—a Roman soldier's experience. Each of them was searching for an end to their personal darkness. And each of them found the Light of the world in God's gift of His Son, Jesus Christ.

It was beautiful. It was unique. And Jennifer knew it contained life-changing seeds of power. No wonder Dan was so taken with it.

For one brief moment, she ached to try the songs of Mary Magdalene. She knew in her heart that her voice was right for the music. But just as quickly, she reminded herself that her voice wasn't the problem. It was her spirit that could no longer sing.

12

On Friday evening, fifteen minutes before the beginning of the radiothon, Jennifer sat in the lounge, staring vacantly outside.

It had been what Dan called a "mizzling" day. The morning had been dreary and oppressively humid; the rest of the day had been even gloomier. A fine drizzle of rain was now beginning to dampen the evening—and Jennifer's mood.

She would have given almost anything at this point for even a few hours of untroubled sleep and an entire day of peace and quiet, a day in which she had to do nothing but simply—think.

Certainly, she had a few things to think about. But the one thing she really *wanted* to think about—*needed* to think about—had to be pushed onto the back burner of her mind, at least for now. How could she hope to be objective about the fact that a man had recently declared he loved her—and had asked her to marry him—when she was in the midst of a thirty-six hour physical and emotional blitz; when her daily routine consisted of peeping toms and pickup truck assaults; and when the man she loved was being hounded by a psychopath?

With a heavy sigh, she turned her attention back to the moment. What she had to do first was to get through this weekend. Try as she would, she was unable to shake the chilling premonition that somewhere a time bomb was ticking madly away, a bomb which could explode at any second.

Although she dreaded leaving Dan, she was thankful and relieved that on Sunday afternoon she'd be going home for a couple of days. She needed time away from the station—perhaps she also needed time away from Dan. Most of all, she needed time to think.

Glancing out the window again, she saw a patrol car park in the station's lot and a policeman approach the sidewalk to the front door. An officer would be at the station throughout the weekend. That should have been a reassuring feeling, but at the moment it didn't seem to help very much.

She drained the last of her coffee from the bottom of the cup and rubbed the back of her neck. With a grim smile, she decided she was beginning to feel a little like the victim in a science fiction story she'd read years ago about a man who had been imprisoned in a room with walls that were slowly moving inward, as well as a rising tide of water that was gradually seeping up through an opening in the floor. The victim knew he would eventually be crushed by the walls or drown in the water; his primary problem, as he saw it, was deciding which peril he would worry about first.

That's it, kid. It's twilight zone time . . . better go to work.

Dan and Sunny came into the lounge just as Jennifer rose from her chair. She noticed that he looked disgustingly fresh other than his red-rimmed eyes. He was wearing a teal blue polo shirt and an unwrinkled pair of pleated canvas pants, and the man didn't even look tired. She glanced down at her own outfit, a hasty, last-minute selection she'd had to settle on this afternoon when she realized that most of her clothes were in the laundry basket—unlaundered. Her plum colored pullover was a size too big and tended to hang in a lopsided slouch over her waist, and her gray cords were too comfortably stretched out to look neat.

"Jennifer?"

"Be with you in a minute. Soon as I finish sticking pins in my arm to see if I'm still alive."

His grin was affectionate and understanding. "You didn't

145

sleep either?" Dan was to have napped on the couch in his office while Jennifer rested at home for three hours late that afternoon.

"Not really. But why is it that I look like a displaced bag lady while you look as if you've been posing for catalog ads?"

"What kind of catalog ads?"

"Oh, you know the ones, where a guy with perfect hair and perfect teeth is leaning back on a fencepost with his face lifted to the wind while he watches a gorgeous white stallion gallop joyfully through the heather on the hill."

"I notice you didn't say anything about a perfect nose."

"You noticed, huh?"

She studied his face, unable to stop a nudge of tenderness that made her heart turn over. "So—how are you, boss?" she asked him softly.

He shrugged. "Okay. I rested a little."

"Good thing, since we have the first shift. Speaking of which, we'd better be getting to the studio."

Dan yawned deeply and followed her out the door. "Katharine said she put a fresh pot of coffee and cups in the studio. We must look pretty bad."

"Nah. Batman and Robin, in control as usual. C'mon, let's go wake up Shepherd Valley."

"We'd better wake up each other first."

Dan and Jennifer stayed on the air until eleven that night, then yielded to Gabe and Jay Regan for three hours. As they walked down the hall from the studio, Dan told Jennifer about a phone call he'd had that afternoon.

The supervisor at the County Children's Home, Mrs. Grayson, had called to advise Dan that they'd had a recent telephone inquiry about adopting a special child. The couple was interested in an older child, not an infant, and specifically wanted a boy.

They stopped at the door of Jennifer's office, and she

146

stared up at him with concern. "Are they thinking of—"

"Jason," he said with a brief nod. "Mrs. Grayson said she'd like to talk with me about it before she interviewed the couple. She wanted me to come in today or tomorrow, but when I explained about the radiothon, she offered to come up to the house Sunday afternoon."

Jennifer could tell that he was severely shaken by this unexpected news. "You're upset, aren't you?"

He bent down to release Sunny from her harness, then stood and leaned against the doorframe of Jennifer's office.

"To tell you the truth, I'm not exactly sure *how* I feel right now." He crossed his arms over his chest and thought for a moment. "I just want whatever's best for Jason," he explained softly. "And I've never really thought that living with me would be all that great for him. A single parent—who's also handicapped—" He shrugged meaningfully. "I've never been too sure he wouldn't be just as well off at the Home."

A faint, sad smile touched his lips, then quickly faded. "Can I ask you something? Just supposing you might agree to marry me—how would you feel about an instant son?" Hearing her sharp intake of breath, he quickly added, "Does Jason still make you uncomfortable?"

"I don't—it isn't that he makes me uncomfortable," Jennifer stammered. "I just feel so *sorry* for him! Dan, we can't talk about this now—"

"I know," he assured her quickly. "I'm not being fair to you. One crisis at a time is enough, right?" His smile was tender as he reached out to gently smooth her hair away from her forehead. "Tired?"

"Mm. Not me. I'm past fatigue. I'm now into the zonk stage."

"The what?"

"Zonk. Total collapse. The mind shuts down but the

147

mouth goes on."

"Oh. Like the way Gabe is all the time."

"Exactly."

He nodded and started to turn away. "I'll have someone call you in about three hours."

"Gently, Daniel. Tell them to be sure and call me very, very gently." A distant rumble interrupted her in mid-sentence. "What was that?"

"What was what?"

"That noise. It rumbled."

"*That* noise?" he asked right after another low growl of thunder echoed far away. "I believe," he said sagely, "that's the sound of an approaching storm."

"A *thunderstorm?* At this time of year? We had snow a few days ago!"

"You're in the mountains now, love. The temperature can move up—as it has over the last few hours—or down real fast. It's not unusual for us to have some nifty storms this time of year, once it starts to warm up."

"Ugh." She shivered.

"What's wrong?"

"Nothing," she said quickly, her voice a half-tone higher than usual.

"No," he drawled softly. "I don't believe it. Not my little rebel."

"What?"

"You're afraid of storms."

"Who said I'm afraid of storms? Did I say I'm afraid of storms?"

"You *are*, aren't you?" He brushed the knuckles of one hand lightly under her chin.

She shrugged, trying to keep her voice light. "I don't exactly *like* storms, I suppose, but I wouldn't say I'm *afraid* of them."

"I see." He grinned down at her and tapped her lightly

under the chin once more. "What *would* you say?"

"Terrified," she said after a second. "I'd probably say terrified."

He shook his head in disbelief. "Well, I don't think this one is going to bother you too much. Once you hit that couch, honey, I doubt that even a good old-fashioned West Virginia thunderstorm is going to keep you awake." He tousled her hair affectionately. "Now go on—sack out while you can."

Dan's last thought before drifting off to a restless, troubled sleep was that maybe he'd been wrong after all. Maybe the radiothon wasn't going to bring the creep out from under his rock. Maybe nothing would happen. Maybe none of it had been anything more than someone's twisted idea of a prank. Maybe he needn't worry about the rest of the weekend . . . .

And then he was on the mountain road again . . . but this time it was different, totally different. The dream propelled him at a dizzying speed past the headlights, past the crunch of metal, past his terrified scream . . . He saw the zigzag of color again, like last time . . . He knew he was dreaming, but he couldn't stop it, couldn't stop the car or the dream or even slow things down . . . He was slammed against the wheel, tossed back and forth against the seat, then against the wheel again . . . and the truck just kept right on coming, closer, closer, coming faster than ever before . . . There was a face—no, it was only an open mouth, no face, just someone screaming at him in anger . . . or in fear . . . and then he was back at the beginning . . . It was starting all over again, and he knew what was going to happen . . . He'd feel the pain and the mind-freezing terror again and again . . . He had to stop the dream or it was going to kill him this time . . . The truck wasn't going to take his sight, it was going to take his life, and he had to stop it . . . *No, he couldn't stop it, there was something he had to see, there was something he'd forgotten and it was desperately*

149

important that he remember . . . now, right now . . . He had to go a little closer, even let himself be hurt, so this time he'd remember, this time he would know . . . .

"Dan! Daniel! Wake up! Dan!" Jennifer was shaking him gently. She took his perspiration soaked face between her hands and held him, trying to stop him from thrashing back and forth on the couch. "It's all right . . . you're just dreaming, Dan. It's all right, I'm here . . . it's all right now."

Dan threw an arm over his face to shield himself from the pain, to stop the truck. Suddenly he felt his hand strike something—

"Jennifer?"

"Yes," she sighed with relief. "Are you all right, Dan?" She ignored the light blow to her face, wrapping her arms as tightly as she could around him and burying her face against his shoulder, her entire body shaking almost as hard as his. "You must have had a terrible dream."

He couldn't answer her yet, couldn't quite focus his mind. He knew he was with Jennifer, but where? He blinked his eyes once, then again. It was still dark, he couldn't see.

Then he remembered. And the memory hit him with the cold thump of sick reality, just as it had every morning for over five years now. He couldn't see because he was blind. He wasn't going to see anything ever again.

He let her hold him, secretly drawing what calm he could from her, allowing himself to be soothed by her. He had always been alone after the dream. There was never anyone to comfort him, to ease his night terrors. With grateful relief, he let her hold him and murmur softly to him and gentle him . . . until he could face the darkness again. All the while he wondered what it was that he needed to remember and if it really *was* important.

13

By Saturday night Dan knew what he had to do. Even though there hadn't been so much as a minor incident during the radiothon, which would end tomorrow morning, all his instincts told him there was more to come. And he still believed this weekend would somehow trigger the climax of the campaign of terror that had been mounted against him.

He had decided to go on the offensive. He wanted the end of this thing to come while Jennifer was safely out of harm's way. She would leave by noon tomorrow to visit her family in Athens. That meant he had two days to take the initiative, to incite his enemy to make a move.

He thought he knew how to do it. But he would have to wait a few hours. It wouldn't do to give his tormentor too much time. He had to be sure Jennifer was gone from Shepherd Valley before the final explosion.

The man in the pickup truck sat staring at the side of the radio station, his view distorted by the rain pouring steadily off the windshield. Every now and then his pale, angry eyes would flick back and forth with the halting, noisy scrape and slide of the windshield wipers; but mostly he stared straight ahead.

Anticipation quickened his phlegmy breathing, and occasionally he choked and coughed. Then he would roll down the window a few inches and toss a half-smoked cigarette outside onto the saturated ground, immediately pulling another from the pack in his jacket pocket. Squeezing it tightly between his shaking, nicotine-stained fingers, he would squint as the smoke from the match burned his eyes.

It was late, but the brick building was only dimly lighted. There were no more than half a dozen cars in the parking lot, including the black Cherokee that belonged to the station, the Terry woman's Honda, and Denton's Thunderbird. And a police cruiser.

He raised one side of his mouth in an angry scowl as his gaze fastened on the patrol car. He hadn't counted on the police staying this long. He had waited all evening, his pickup safely hidden behind the brush and pine trees on the hill. But the cruiser was still there. He might just as well go home for the night. His chest tightened painfully and the sour taste in his mouth grew even more rancid when he decided to leave.

He fiddled with the radio dial. Even this close, the station was laced with static; the night was sparked with electricity. A gospel song came over the air, and he turned it off with a snap.

Kaine hadn't talked for a long time; he wondered what he was doing in there. Not that it mattered. He wasn't going to be able to finish him tonight. He'd have to wait till tomorrow. But that was all right. Kaine would be worn out by then. And he wouldn't be surrounded by so many people. Maybe it would be even better. Easier. Yeah, he'd get him at home. Alone.

He eased the pickup out of the grove as quietly as possible, glancing furtively in the rearview mirror for one last look at the station. As he drove down the hill, his tires made a slashing noise on the old pavement brick. Once he was well away from the station, he turned the radio on again. The gospel song had ended, and that wise mouth Denton was gabbing. He held his arm up close to his face, trying to catch what little light there was from the streetlight so he could see the time. It was almost midnight.

Dan and Gabe took a long drivetime in the early morning

152

hours, insisting that Jennifer sleep a while since she was going to be leaving for Athens later. She came back into the studio at four that morning and relieved Gabe.

She and Dan talked about the tremendous success of the radiothon while their mikes were closed. They had already gone over their financial goal, and at least four other reporting stations had done the same. They both agreed it had been worth all the effort.

At seven o'clock, on the last hour of the radiothon, Jennifer went to her office to brief Jay Regan and Gabe, who would be handling the regular Sunday broadcasting. Dan waited until he heard the studio door close with a soft thud and the last record sound its final chord. Then he opened his mike.

He took a deep, steadying breath, touched his headset briefly, and began to speak.

" . . . And now a word for my friend in the noisy pickup truck." He paused, then went on. "I got your package. And all your messages. Now I've got a message for *you*." His voice was level, cold, and hard, even though he spoke softly into the mike.

"I know who you are, man. And I know what you're doing, and why you're doing it. So let's stop playing games. I've known about you, who you are, what you want, for a long time now. And after this weekend is over, the police will know everything I know." He hesitated for an instant, then added, *"The blind man is callin' your bluff, pal."*

He turned off his mike, quickly cued up another record, and said a brief, silent prayer for forgiveness . . . .

You and I both know I'm faking, Lord . . . I don't have the faintest idea in the world who this nut is, but I've got to make him show himself while Jennifer's gone . . . I've got this awful feeling that he might try to get at me through her . . . I'm sorry, Lord, but I don't know what else to do . . . I can't shake the feeling that I'm running out of time, that he's closing in . . . I have to force his hand now, before someone besides me gets hurt. . . .

The thin, angry man hurled his coffee cup across the room, his eyes blazing as the pieces shattered on the wall and fell to the floor. *Big-mouthed ape!* Who did he think he was, anyway? Talking to the whole town like that!

He wiped his watering eyes on a dirty sleeve and slumped down onto the cracked plastic seat of a battered kitchen chair. So he'd been right all along. Kaine *did* know. How long had he known? When had he remembered? Probably hadn't been too long. He'd have done something about it otherwise.

Well, it was a good thing he'd planned to take him out. Once he blabbed to the police, that would finish it. They'd never believe *me*, not against that blind churcher! The whole town thinks he's some kind of a saint or something. They'd listen to anything he said, just because he's such a *big, important man!*

Well, they wouldn't be listening to him after today. He was going to shut his big mouth for good. Then he wouldn't have to listen to him anymore. And he wouldn't have to worry anymore. Because no one else would ever know. He'd be safe. Finally safe.

14

Dan missed her already, and it was only one o'clock. Jennifer hadn't even been gone three hours yet, but her absence was like a hole in his heart.

If it hurt this much when she left him for two days, how would he live with it if she refused to marry him? If he had to settle for living on the outside fringes of her life forever? She was as important to him as breathing by now. He needed her to live. Otherwise, he'd just be taking up space.

Oh, Lord, you know how much I love her . . . and I've let myself believe that you brought her into my life for me to love . . . to marry . . . but what if I'm wrong? What if I'm wrong?

Would she talk to her father and brother about him? Would they try to discourage her from getting involved with a blind man? With a dart of anxiety, he realized he couldn't blame them if they did. If Jennifer were his daughter or his sister, he might do the same. How many men *would* encourage someone they loved to marry a person with his handicap?

He sank down onto the piano bench, letting his fingers strum idly over the keys with no purpose other than to try to fill the emptiness of his house with sound . . . any sound. It seemed strange to be alone. Of course, it wouldn't last. But he was glad of it for now, at least.

He had tried to put Gabe's mind at rest about leaving him for the afternoon, insisting that he needed him to take over the station for the rest of the day. He'd promised to have Lyss or his dad pick him up and take him down to his folks' house for dinner later, after the appointment with Mrs. Grayson. Only then had Gabe agreed to stay at the station until time for evening worship at church.

Dan had already called the police and told them not to bother having the house watched this afternoon, that he'd be gone after two. So now he had nothing to do but wait for Mrs. Grayson. He had every intention of leaving the house as soon as she did. Earlier he had almost convinced himself to spend the afternoon alone, waiting for his psychotic friend to make a move. But he'd finally admitted to himself that he wasn't that brave. Or that stupid.

In fact, he now realized with a sense of defeat, his idea to lure the man out into the open had been full of holes from the beginning. He'd been so determined to force his hand while Jennifer was gone that he'd forgotten a couple of things. If this nut came after him while he was alone, there was very little he could do to stop him. He had Sunny with him, but he wouldn't know where the guy was or what he was doing.

On the other hand, while his first thought had been to protect Jennifer, he didn't want anyone *else* who happened to be with him getting hurt either. After thinking it through, he became extremely discouraged and irritated with himself and decided he should just leave the house as soon as he could.

Preoccupied by his thoughts when the doorbell rang, he misstepped a couple of inches on his way to answer it, stubbing his toe against the rolltop desk. When he opened the door for the superintendent he was surprised to realize she had Jason with her.

"I hope you don't mind my bringing him along, Dan," she said as they entered. "But he's missed you terribly the last few days, and I thought it might be good for him to spend a few minutes with you."

"That's fine," Dan responded after a slight hesitation. "He can play with Sunny while we talk." In truth, he would have preferred it if Jason hadn't come. He was tense and edgy enough without having to worry about something happening to the child. But he was here, so Dan did his best not to communicate his anxiety to Mrs. Grayson or the boy.

After cuffing him playfully a few times and giving him a big hug, Dan sent Jason and Sunny up to the loft to play.

"I'm sorry I haven't been able to spend any time with him this week," Dan said as they sat down in the living room. "I explained about the radiothon—"

"Yes, I understand. But Jason has become terribly attached to you, Daniel, and he's unhappy when he's away from you for any length of time. That's why I wanted to talk with you."

Dan remained silent while she told him about the inquiry she'd had from the prospective adoptive couple. "I just wanted to be completely sure you weren't interested in adopting Jason yourself before going any further."

Surprised, Dan hesitated for a moment before answering. "I *would* be interested—very interested—if I weren't blind . . . and single."

Mrs. Grayson nodded to herself. "I understand that. But I've seen you and the boy together, Daniel. Quite frankly, I have my doubts that a healthy, physically perfect couple can meet Jason's needs any better than you can—if as well."

Caught off guard by her attitude, Dan wasn't sure what to say. "There would be a lot of problems," he began.

"There are *always* a lot of problems when you become a parent," she said with a smile. "But I've worked with children and adoptive parents for years, Daniel, and I've seen some staggering problems overcome by nothing more than plenty of love and commonsense."

"I *do* love the boy," Dan said thoughtfully. "And I'd jump at the chance to have him with me if I thought I wouldn't be cheating him."

"If you should decide to consider it, it might be advisable for you to fill out a preliminary application. This wouldn't bind you to anything," she assured him quickly. "But it would allow us to get started on a home study and reference check for you. And," she added meaningfully, "it would allow me to place you in the file for consideration as a prospective parent. In addition to others, of course."

Dan rubbed one hand over his chin, then gave a small nod of his head and smiled. "There's someone I'd like to discuss this with, Mrs. Grayson. Would I be hurting my chances any if I waited until the middle of the week to get an application in process?"

The superintendent encouraged him to take his time and consider any decision carefully. She then rose from her chair to leave. When they called Jason and Sunny to come downstairs, the boy begged Dan to stay. "Just while Mrs. Grayson does her errands, Dan. Please? I'll be real quiet."

Dan was uncomfortable about being alone with the boy right now, but he couldn't explain that to Jason. When Mrs. Grayson said she wouldn't be gone any more than an hour, he agreed that Jason could stay until she returned.

Sunny and Jason followed Dan outside when he walked Mrs. Grayson to her car. She advised Dan not to say anything to Jason that would give him false hope, but did suggest the two of them might at least discuss their feelings about each other.

After her car pulled away, Dan unhooked Sunny's harness. "Let's give her a few minutes out here, Jason, since the rain has stopped. She's been cooped up inside the station with me all weekend."

The afternoon was heavy with a clammy, thick humidity. But it was warm. And, at least for the moment, it wasn't raining. Sunny ventured a few feet away, then returned to check on them before trotting off to sniff around the wet grass again. Jason continued to hold Dan's hand as they walked around the front yard. He enjoyed being Dan's guide and they always made a game of it.

"You know, sport, there's something I'd like to talk about for a minute, okay?" He tousled the boy's light hair affectionately.

"What, Dan?" Jason was far more interested in what Sunny was doing.

Dan proceeded to tell him simply and sincerely, how he felt about him. "You're very special to me, Jason. I like being with you, and I love you very much. In fact, you're like my own little boy. That's how much I care about you. Do you understand that?"

They stopped walking, and Dan felt Jason clasp his hand even tighter. "I love you, too, Dan," he said simply. He surprised Dan with his immediate, sober response and his perception. "And I wish you *were* my daddy."

"Why is that, Jason?" He felt a little tug at his heart when he heard how small and serious Jason sounded.

"So I could stay with you forever."

After a pause, Dan asked, "You'd like that, would you, Jason? To stay with me, even though you might never have a mother?"

Jason considered that for a moment. "I'd like to have a mother, too. But I wouldn't be sad without one if you were my daddy." Then something else occurred to him. "Maybe Jennifer would like to be my mother. I think she likes me. And I *know* she likes you!"

Dan's grin was a quick flash of pleasure at Jason's words. "You think so, huh?" Laughing, he picked the boy up and swung him to his shoulder, then set him lightly to his feet.

Hearing their laughter, Sunny bounded over to see what she was missing, but stopped suddenly and turned at the sound only her ears had sensed.

Her instinct, born of long, intensive training, years of experience—and immeasurable love—was to immediately ignore her own desire to play, even to ignore the fact that she wasn't on her harness. Moving like a golden fireball, she

159

hurled herself directly at Dan.

Sunny took the first bullet in her side. Jason, thinking the retriever wanted to play, jumped to grab her front paws. He caught the second bullet in his abdomen.

Dan heard Sunny yelp like a hurt pup, but Jason went down with no more than a surprised sob. Only after the second explosion did he realize what he'd heard. Both shots had been from a rifle. And both shots had found a target.

With the third explosion, Dan, reacting by raw instinct, pitched to the ground in an attempt to remove himself as a target. At the same time, he urgently choked out Jason's name. Then Sunny's.

No sound broke the deadly quiet on the mountain. He could hear nothing but the pounding of his heart as he lay, silently waiting. He forced himself to lie perfectly still, hoping the sniper would think he'd been hit.

He'll eventually come to be sure he got me. The thought froze him with panic. For an instant he thought he was going to be sick. He felt his skin grow quickly cold and wet with perspiration. He swallowed hard against the hot taste of bile rising in his throat. He wanted desperately to reach out and grope for Sunny or Jason but he didn't dare.

I'm totally helpless . . . I'm a sitting duck, there's nothing I can do to stop him, no way I can help them . . . Oh, Lord, are they dead? Did he kill Jason and Sunny? What can I do, I don't even know where he is, where the shots came from . . . they might still be alive . . . but they'll bleed to death if I don't get help somehow . . . help me . . . merciful God, help me . . . .

He stiffened, held his breath, unable to believe what he heard. Was he imagining it? Suddenly his entire body began to tremble. It was real. It was a car. There was a car coming up the mountain. He clenched his teeth together until the tension hurt his jaw, forcing himself not to move, not to cry out. It couldn't be Mrs. Grayson coming back; it was too soon. *A truck?* He tensed even more, then melted with relief. No. Closer now, he knew it was a car. A familiar car. His dad's Lincoln. *Thank You . . . oh, my dear Lord, thank you . . . .*

But then he realized—he had to warn his dad . . . he couldn't let him pull in the driveway and get out of the car without knowing . . . he had to warn him.

He waited until the solid, powerful sound of the big engine slowed as it turned into the driveway, waited until the exact instant the ignition died before pushing himself to his knees and hauling himself upright to wave his hands and shout a warning.

15

The steady downpour of rain had been with her since she left Athens, turning the road outside her windshield into an eerie, distorted rivulet. But Jennifer had cried so hard since her troubled, hasty departure that she no longer knew whether it was her tears or the rainstorm making it so difficult to see the road.

Lyss's call that evening, coming only hours after Jennifer had arrived in Athens, had shaken her so badly that her dad had begged her to stay overnight and leave in the morning. But she had hurriedly thrown her things back into her overnighter, kissed him and Loren goodbye, and started for West Virginia.

The ache at the back of her neck was nothing compared to the ache in her heart as she remembered her conversation with Dan's sister.

"Dan told me not to call you, but Gabe said I should." Lyss's voice had been frightened and strained when she relayed the bad news about Jason and Sunny.

Jennifer could still feel the fear that had knotted her stomach when she'd heard the details of the shooting.

"So if Gabe hadn't got worried when Dan didn't answer the phone, your dad would never have gone up there."

"That's right," Lyss had responded. "Gabe had called twice, but apparently Dan and Jason were outside. He was just uneasy enough about Dan that he decided to ask Dad to check on him."

"Thank the Lord for that," Jennifer had said softly into the phone. "But we still don't know who the man is." The thought that he was out there, free to try again, made Jennifer physically ill with dread.

162

"No. The police said the shots were from a high-powered hunting rifle. They think he was on the upper side of the hill and took off when he saw Dad's car. He'd have been out of sight within seconds."

"How serious is Jason?"

Lyss hesitated a moment. "He's been unconscious since the shooting. The bullet wound wasn't deep, but apparently he hit his head on a rock when he fell. He has a concussion. Dad and Baker Ferguson are both taking care of him. They think it may be several hours before we really know how he's doing."

"And Sunny?"

"She's at the vet's. She was hit in the side when she jumped against Dan. It's touch and go, but they think she's going to be all right."

"Dan must be half-crazy by now. Lyss—you're *sure* he's all right?"

A deep, troubled sigh came over the telephone line. "Physically, he's all right, yes." Jennifer had suddenly realized that Lyss was crying softly. "But he's so—*destroyed*, Jennifer! He's blaming himself for the whole thing!"

Lyss had explained then what Dan had admitted to his family earlier, that he'd deliberately tried to bait his tormentor into making a move while Jennifer was out of town.

Horrified that he'd taken it upon himself to do something so dangerous in order to protect her, Jennifer had remained silent while Lyss continued.

"You're not going to find the same Dan you left, Jennifer," she had warned. "I haven't seen him this way since the accident."

With the back of one hand, Jennifer now wiped tiredly at her eyes, squinting against the monotonous swipe of the windshield wipers. Lyss's final words made her think sadly of something her dad had said after she had told him about Dan earlier that day, before she knew about the shootings.

163

"You know, Jenny—" no one but her father ever called her that—"I think the secret of your Daniel's remarkable spirit is that he's placed it in the hands of a loving Lord, a Lord who's far, far wiser than any of us. Daniel has allowed God to work His will in whatever way He chooses . . . even through a tragedy like blindness."

Steven Terry's dark brown eyes, so much like his daughter's, had studied Jennifer for a long time. "That's how it was with your mother, too. Even in those last few days at the hospital, just before she died, she allowed the Lord to use her illness—to use *her*—to make a difference for others."

His eyes had misted and his voice had been unsteady as he explained. "You need to know, Jenny, that there are at least half a dozen lives somewhere out there that would never have been changed if it hadn't been for your mother's faith." He had paused a moment before going on. "I believe with all my heart that, if she could, your mother would tell you to look for the glory in things, not the grief."

It was well after eleven when she drove into town and raining so hard she could just barely make out the red lights of the radio tower on the hill. For some inexplicable reason, the sight of the tower saddened her. The lights always made her think of Dan. He was so much a part of the station—and the station so much a part of him. It was that way with Jason and Sunny, too—they had become important, even vital to Dan's life.

With a peculiar feeling of dismay, Jennifer thought it was almost as though Dan were being cut off from all the things that really mattered most to him.

She pressed the gas pedal a little harder. Suddenly it seemed to be absolutely essential that she get to Dan as quickly as possible.

She found him at the hospital with Lyss and Gabe. Jennifer stopped short for a moment when she got off the

164

elevator on the second floor. She could see the three of them sitting in the small lounge at the far end of the hall. Taking a deep breath to steady herself, she began walking down the dimly lighted corridor toward them.

Gabe stood up as soon as he saw her and gave her a weak smile. Lyss also got to her feet, glancing from Jennifer to Dan, who sat woodenly on a blue, plastic-covered chair, his head buried wearily in both hands.

He raised his head when he heard her approaching steps. Jennifer thought uneasily that his expression wasn't so much surprise as it was indifference. "Jennifer?" His tone was flat.

Now that she was close enough to get a good look at him, Jennifer caught her breath in alarm at what she saw. She found it difficult to respond to Lyss's welcoming hug or Gabe's quick squeeze of her hand. Instead, she could only stare with concern at Dan. His hair needed combing, his light blue sweatshirt was spotted with what appeared to be grass stain, and his face was haggard, engraved with stark, grim lines of fatigue and worry. Other than voicing her name, he made no move to acknowledge her presence.

She swallowed hard and forced herself to stoop down beside him. "Dan—are you all right?" She covered his hands with her own, but he held himself rigidly unmoving, offering only a small nod to her question.

"Jason—how is he?"

When he didn't answer, she looked up at Gabe and then Lyss, who shook her head and replied forlornly, "No change. He's still unconscious."

Returning her gaze to Dan, Jennifer studied him, waiting for some sign of welcome. Finally he spoke. "Who called you?"

"Lyss. She knew I'd want to be here."

"She told you what happened then," he said heavily.

"Yes. Oh, Dan . . . I'm so sorry. I know how much Jason

165

means to you. And Sunny." She paused, then tried to reassure him. "They'll be all right, Dan."

He pulled away from her and slumped back against the chair. "All this," he said thickly, "and we still don't even know who he is."

"But we'll find out," Jennifer insisted, getting to her feet. She turned to Gabe. "Don't the police know anything yet?"

With a look of abject frustration, Gabe shook his head. "Not a clue."

Just then Lucas Kaine, a big, silver-haired model of his son, walked out of a room a few doors down and approached them. Jennifer thought Lucas appeared to be as exhausted as Dan. But his eyes lighted when he saw her standing there. He immediately went to her and took her by the hand.

"Jennifer, I'm so glad you're here." He darted a quick glance at his son. "There's no change, Dan. I just checked Jason again."

His look took in everyone at the same time. "I think all of you should go home now and get some rest." He held up a restraining hand when Lyss started to object. "Jason will be monitored throughout the night. That's all we can do right now." He hesitated, then added sternly, "You look terrible—every one of you. You're not doing anyone any good this way."

He then turned a meaningful look on Gabe. "I want Dan to stay with us tonight. Will you take him out to the house? I'm going to stick around here for another hour or so."

Gabe hesitated and looked uneasily at Dan, who simply shook his head in a short, negative gesture. "I'm staying with Jason. In case he wakes up."

With an uncertain glance at Lucas, Gabe closed the distance between himself and Dan. "Dan, you're not going to accomplish anything except to wear yourself out," he told his friend.

"I'm staying here tonight," Dan said flatly.

166

With a tired sigh, Lucas met Gabe's eyes and shrugged. "All right. If that's what you want, son."

"Take me to the room, please, Gabe," Dan said dully.

Gabe looked at Dan with surprise, as if he'd just become aware of Sunny's absence. He reached out tentatively to take Dan's arm. "Sure, buddy. C'mon."

Surprised and disturbed, Jennifer watched as Dan docilely allowed his friend to lead him down the hall to Jason's room. He hadn't even told her goodnight. She had to fight back tears of hurt as she watched the two of them walk away. Dan's shoulders were slumped, his steps uncertain and shuffling.

For the first time since she'd met him, Jennifer thought with sick despair, Dan looked . . . blind.

16

It took only two days for Jennifer to see what Lyss had meant when she'd told her to expect "a different Daniel."

On the surface, he seemed to be following a very ordinary routine, doing what might be expected of him. He went to work; he went home, although "home" had temporarily become his parents' house; and he went to visit Jason at the hospital and Sunny at the vet's—usually with Jennifer or Gabe. Jason remained unresponsive, though Jennifer knew that Dan spent hours at his side talking with the boy as though he could hear every word being said to him. Sunny, however, was recovering. She now recognized her visitors and would nuzzle Dan's hand lovingly each time he gently touched her face.

To an outsider, it would seem as if little had changed. To Jennifer, it seemed that her whole world had changed. Dan had become an empty reflection of his former self. He was like a vacant, arid chamber lined with closed doors and no windows. His uncanny sensitivity, his sustaining sense of humor, his upbeat wisdom and warmth had vanished.

He came to the station, but stayed out of the studio, remaining in his office to work behind a closed door. He ate most of his meals alone at his desk, and Jennifer noted with concern that much of his food ended up in the wastecan. If he happened to venture into the lounge when others were present, he sat quietly drinking his coffee, seemingly unaware of the conversation going on around him. To Jennifer he was courteous but never warm, polite but never personal. He had become her employer—professional, distant, and distracted.

The worst of it was that he had taken to wearing dark

glasses and walking with a cane, neither of which Jennifer had ever seen him do before now and both of which made her want to cry for him and scream at him at the same time.

The first time she saw him with the cane and glasses, she was unable to keep silent. She tried to be tactful when she commented on them, but she needn't have bothered. His reply was wooden and indifferent, as though he had scarcely registered her remark.

"They help to identify me as blind," he'd said with a small shrug. "Without Sunny, I'm awkward. I stumble sometimes, bump into things. The cane helps me avoid crashing into people, and the glasses let them know I can't see."

She had offered a very cautious observation that Sunny's absence was only temporary, a few weeks at most. He had said nothing, merely waiting until she finished speaking. Then he had walked on down the hall, the offensive cane monotonously tap-tapping in front of him as he went.

She had tried to talk to Gabe about Dan, but he was as upset and frustrated as Jennifer. "I *hate* seeing him with that cane and those glasses!" he had exploded the day before in the lounge. "He used a cane before he went to Seeing Eye and got Sunny. When he came back with her, he said he'd *never* use that 'despicable cane' again. Those were his exact words. It isn't that there's anything wrong with using the cane or the glasses—it's just the memories attached to them that bother me so much."

Jennifer cautiously tried to return their relationship to what it had been. But every effort she made turned into a miserable failure. Her attempts at humor bombed hopelessly; her not-so-subtle hints about the way he was avoiding her seemed to fall on deaf ears. Dan had shut her out, along with everyone else. And there seemed to be nothing she could do about it.

By Wednesday evening, Jennifer was physically exhausted, but her mind was stuck on fast-forward. Combined with Dan's bewildering and painful rejection was the continual worry about Jason and Sunny, not to mention the ever-present awareness that there was still a lunatic out there bent on hurting Dan—or worse.

Right now she was finding it difficult to think about anything except Dan. She had left the station earlier than usual, bogged down in a black depression that was growing worse by the minute.

Driven by sheer desperation to find something—anything—that would help her comprehend what was going on inside of him, she was now sitting at her kitchen table, hunched intently over Dan's journal. She didn't know what it was she really hoped to find—perhaps some kind of magic key that would unlock the complex secrets of his heart so she could meet him where he was and understand what he was going through.

Before now, she had scanned a few pages but had been reluctant to devote the time and concentration necessary to plumb the depths of emotion and insight these pages contained. This evening, however, she had once more begun on page one, stopping only when her attention was captured, a few pages later, by something in his notes, a thought that reminded her of one of the songs in *Daybreak*.

At the same time, a splash of color tucked in the back lining of the notebook caught her eye, and she pulled out what appeared to be a book jacket. She studied it curiously for a moment, then drew in a sharp, stunned breath. What she held in her hands was the cover to the published musical score of *Daybreak*. It clearly identified Daniel Kaine as the composer of both lyrics and music. She sat staring at the bright design of the cover for several moments, her gaze unable to leave Dan's name.

Finally, she reached behind her to the portable tape player on the counter. The demo for *Daybreak* was still in place, and she pushed the play button to start it. Then she returned to the journal.

For the next few hours, she was held captive by this extraordinarily personal, penetrating glimpse of the mind and heart of a man she was only now beginning to understand.

It was an intensely painful process. Her eyes often blurred by tears, Jennifer followed the spiritual and emotional journey of a man groping his way toward the reality of a loving God, a man seeking sanity in the midst of a nightmare, hope in the midst of despair, and faith in the midst of destruction. Long after the clock on the City Building had struck nine and the last light of evening had turned to darkness, Jennifer continued to trace Dan's steps, to walk with him through the long and dreary midnight of his soul.

She even found herself praying with him, not the quick, routine type of prayer her devotions had degenerated to over the past few years, but now the plea of an injured child in the first throes of recognizing her own need for healing.

She was there with him, beside his hospital bed years before, when his horror-stricken brain refused to acknowledge reality but continued to anesthetize itself to time and place. . . . *In dark places He has made me dwell, like those who have long been dead . . . .*

She sat by the bed and watched him fight his way through the maze of pain and shock and denial, felt his sickening awareness of being violated, mutilated, and humiliated. . . . *I am the man who has seen affliction . . . He has driven me and made me walk in darkness and not in light . . . He has besieged and encompassed me with bitterness and hardship . . . .*

She smelled his fear and tasted his tears, shared his anger

171

and suffered his defeat until she thought she could no longer bear the haunted labyrinth of his heart. . . . *He has made me desolate . . . my soul has been rejected from peace; I have forgotten happiness . . . . My strength has perished, and so has my hope from the Lord . . . .*

But she couldn't leave him; by now she was his partner in agony as she saw him fumble his way past utter despair and finally get to his knees, then stand and begin to fight. . . . *I have called you by name; you are Mine! When you pass through the waters, I will be with you; and through the rivers, they will not overflow you. When you walk through the fire, you will not be scorched, nor will the flame burn you . . . .*

She echoed his anguished questions during those first weeks after he left the hospital as he suffered the frustration and humiliation of dependency, and she understood his need for self-defense. . . . *Oh, that I knew where I might find Him . . . I would present my case before Him and fill my mouth with arguments . . . It is God who has made my heart faint, and the Almighty who has dismayed me, but I am not silenced by the darkness, nor deep gloom which covers me . . . .*

Then slowly, and reluctantly, she began to listen with him throughout the weary days and weeks and months of searching as his God spoke and challenged and thundered His truth from the pages of His word. . . . *I am the Lord, and there is no other, the One forming light and creating darkness . . . I am the Lord who does all these . . . Who has given to Me that I should repay him? Whatever is under the whole heaven is Mine . . . .*

Weakly, she knelt with him in the garden of his final battle, waiting and watching as he finally admitted his humanness, his weakness, and his sin. . . . *Who are you, O man, who answers back to God? The thing molded will not say to the* molder, *"Why did you make me like this," will it? Or does not the potter have a right over the clay . . . Behold, like the clay in the potter's hand, so are you in My hand . . . Woe to the one who quarrels with his Maker . . . .*

She fell face down with him in the dust and ashes of his pride as his broken, shattered spirit once and for all acknowledged the truth of his Creator, the sovereignty of his Savior, and the eternity of his Redeemer. . . . *My spirit is broken . . . I have declared that which I did not understand, things too wonderful for me, which I did not know . . . Shall we indeed accept good from God and not accept adversity? . . . I know that my Redeemer lives . . . Though He slay me, I will hope in Him . . . .*

And finally, then, she realized as Daniel had, that he had been weak until the Lord made him strong . . . that he had been afraid until the Lord made him brave . . . that he had been rebellious and angry until the Lord made him gentle and kind . . . that he was no more than what his Lord had made him, and the best of what he now was had come out of the fire of affliction.

On these pages born of his pain, she saw his pride, his stubbornness, his rebellion, his fury, his fear, his denial, his doubt, and his weakness. She watched him come to the end of his own resources, humble himself, and acknowledge the majesty and sovereignty of his God. She witnessed a man broken by grief and pain transformed into a restored, whole man of God. . . . *And the Lord blessed the latter days of Job more than his beginning . . . the Lord gave and the Lord has taken away. Blessed be the name of the Lord.*

And then Jennifer knelt and allowed the Lord to begin the same healing and renewing process in her own life, knowing this was what Daniel had meant. This was what he had wanted for her.

She wept and prayed for what seemed like hours, giving

God her anger and rebellion, her confusion and resentment and hopelessness. She gave Him her fractured ego, her shattered dreams, her broken heart. Finally, she felt the pain of her past recede. And then she knew her healing had begun.

While still on her knees, she caught a sharp new glimpse of truth about the man she loved more than life, a truth Dan himself had already tried to convey to her. He was no giant, no spiritual colossus. He was only a man, human and imperfect and subject to the same faults and frailties as she was. He was a wounded hero who had fought on the battleground of his faith—and overcome. Through his loss, he had won; in his weakness, he had become strong; and in his surrender, he had been made much more than a conqueror.

Jennifer had long wondered at the secret of Dan's peace. Now, ever so slowly, that secret began to dawn in the shadows of her mind. Daniel had realized and acknowledged God's absolute right to do with His creation as He willed. And then he had learned to trust the Lord's love enough to surrender his broken heart and his searching soul to that love. In the abyss of his pain, he had finally thrown himself upon the mercy of his God . . . and God had taken the bitter dust of blindness and breathed a new life of faith into being. This was the light that glowed from Daniel Kaine, the light at which others warmed their hearts.

But now his light was flickering and threatening to go out. He was giving in once more to defeat and guilt and despair. She sensed in him a weariness, a tired hopelessness that simply refused to fight another battle. And she understood, even sympathized with his inclination to retreat. Once more the humiliation and despair of dependency had been thrust upon him. Added to that was his loss of pride at being unable to protect those he loved.

Jennifer ached for him. But she couldn't allow him the crutch of guilt or the comfort of self-pity. Somehow she must make him remember what he had tried so desperately to teach her. In her heart, she knew she might well be the only one who could give him the will to stand and fight again.

17

By Friday Jennifer had sorted out her own battle and feelings. She knew it was time to face Dan. It was another odd, unseasonably warm night. The atmosphere was close and almost oppressive with electricity. Thunder drummed faintly in the distance, and inky, thick clouds hung ominously above the valley. Jennifer shuddered and gripped the steering wheel even tighter when the sky suddenly glowed with several random flashes of lightning. There appeared to be a sizable storm moving in from the northwest.

She saw with relief that Dan's house was bathed with light, inside and out. The security light by the garage was on as were the carriage lights on either side of the front door. Inside, the lower level was aglow throughout. The apprehension she'd felt when his mother told her Dan had gone back to his house to spend the weekend faded when she saw a police cruiser parked on one side of the driveway.

Shepherd Valley was small enough that the police force always seemed to be short on manpower. But ever since Jason and Sunny had been shot, they had done their best to assign a patrolman to Dan when he had to be alone for any length of time.

Dan's mother had told Jennifer that he had been extremely restless and depressed all evening. He'd finally insisted on going home so he could swim for a while. "Gabe drove him to the house." Pauline's voice had sounded worried when she continued. "He and Lyss were going to the hospital to see Jason, and they had to stop at the station for a few minutes, too. Then Gabe is going back to Dan's to stay the night."

Jennifer cut the engine and got out of her car, tucked

Dan's journal under her arm and, as an afterthought, tossed her rain slicker over it before hurrying up the driveway to the porch.

Rick, the same patrolman who had been at her house the night she'd had the peeping tom, unlocked the door, leaving the security chain on until he saw Jennifer. He was in uniform, and Jennifer noted uneasily that his hand was touching his holstered service revolver when he opened the door for her to enter.

"Good to see you, Miss Terry," he said politely. "Mrs. Kaine called to tell me you were coming."

Jennifer tossed her yellow slicker over a dining room chair, holding onto the journal.

"Dan's in there," the policeman said, gesturing toward the door that led from the kitchen into the pool area. "Sounds like it's cooking up a storm outside."

Jennifer nodded. "Something's headed this way, I'm afraid." She pushed up the sleeves on her oversized pink sweater and started toward the pool area.

She opened the door slowly and quietly, stopping just inside. Dan was in the water and obviously hadn't heard her enter. Jennifer stood silently, watching him with fascination and remembering Dr. Rodaven's words when he had first told her about Dan's blindness . . . "He was a real power-house in the water."

He still is, Jennifer thought. But she sensed that the power now emanating from him as he thudded through the water in a perfectly executed and precision controlled front crawl was at least partly born of anger and frustration.

She expelled a sharp breath of appreciation as he reached the far end of the pool, did a lightning fast flip turn and roared through the water again. He was approaching her now, and she could see the mixture of anguish and rage contorting his face.

He turned and did another lap, and Jennifer glanced from the man in the water to the two photos on the pool wall— photos which, Dan had told her, his mother had insisted upon hanging. They had been taken at the Olympics the year he won the gold medals for the United States. A younger, beardless Dan was standing in the middle of a beaming huddle consisting of his parents, Gabe and Lyss. He looked flushed with victory and extremely pleased.

Jennifer returned her gaze, now tear-scalded, to the pool. He had stopped in the middle of a stroke and was treading water. The strong emotions that had been playing on his features only a moment before had relaxed to a look of weary resignation.

"Dan—" Jennifer walked around to the side of the pool and stopped.

He jumped with surprise, bobbed up and down in the water a few times, then swam slowly to the side of the pool. "Jennifer?" He hauled himself up out of the water enough to fumble for a white terry cloth robe lying nearby, which Jennifer immediately stooped over to hand him.

He came out of the pool, then shrugged into his robe. "D'you see my towel anywhere?"

Wordlessly, Jennifer retrieved the towel off a nearby aluminum chair and pressed it into his hands.

"What are you doing here?" His guarded tone stopped just short of being rude.

"I—thought maybe we could talk."

His eyes narrowed speculatively as he towel dried his hair. "Something wrong?"

"No," she said quickly, then hesitated before explaining. "I—I thought it was time I gave you an answer." At his puzzled expression, she added, "To your proposal."

He stopped his brisk motions with the towel, his arms suspended for an instant above his head. An expression of disbelieving anger settled over his features, but he remained stonily silent.

Jennifer cleared her throat awkwardly and continued. "You asked me," she said as evenly as possible, "to marry you. Remember?" She held her breath, watching him.

His face darkened, and for a moment he looked bewildered. Then, unbelievably, he began to dry his hair again with slow, steady motions as Jennifer stood there watching, all color draining from her face.

"Go home, Jennifer," he said quietly but not unkindly. "Don't do this. Not now."

"Don't do what?" she asked in a choked, tight voice. "Don't you want my answer?"

"*Just . . . don't.*" His voice was hard with warning. But Jennifer instinctively understood his reaction. He thought she had come out of pity.

She had to remind herself that this was Dan. Not as she had learned to know him and not as she had grown to love him . . . but Dan, nevertheless.

"I see. You weren't serious, then . . . when you asked me to marry you? When you told me you loved me?"

Suddenly she knew she'd hit a nerve. He actually flinched and stopped that inane, monotonous toweling of his hair. "Things are—different now. You know that." He dropped the towel onto the chair beside him, letting his hand dangle loosely at his sides.

It struck Jennifer suddenly that he was much thinner. And she was certain there were lines fanning out from his eyes that hadn't been there a few days ago. "What exactly has changed, Dan? Your feelings about me?"

He turned away from her, but before he did, Jennifer saw his face glaze with pain. "Listen," he began softly, "You don't owe me an answer. Just . . . go home. Please."

"No."

He pivoted around in surprise at her firm reply.

Please, Lord . . . let me get through to him . . . let me reach him, help him . . . please.

"Daniel . . . you said you loved me. Has that changed so quickly?"

"What are you trying to do here?" His voice was a strangled rasp.

"Humiliate myself, apparently," Jennifer replied in a small voice, determined not to cry.

"Jennifer—don't . . . "

"I came to tell you that my answer is yes, Daniel. I want to marry you." She could hear her own weakness in her tremulous words. "Unless, of course, you *have* changed your mind. About us."

She felt a quick stab of hope when she saw a parade of conflicting emotions begin to march across his face. He shook his head in a bemused motion, then lifted a restraining hand as though to stop her from going any further.

"Jennifer, don't do this to me, to yourself, don't—"

"And if you're thinking," she pressed on, determined to hold what small edge of advantage she now had, "that this has anything to do with my feeling sorry for you, forget it." She deliberately sharpened her tone.

He started to reply, but she moved in even harder. "I don't feel sorry for you at all," she said firmly. "In fact, Daniel, if you want the truth, I'm a little angry with you right now."

His heavy, dark brows knit together in a confused frown. "What—"

"I read your journal," she said matter-of-factly. "I'm returning it, by the way. It seems to me that you need to re-read it yourself. I think you've forgotten a few things."

"Now, *listen*—"

He was angry. *Good. At least I've got him feeling*

180

something. That's a start.

She slammed the journal down on the white aluminum table. "What you wrote on those pages, Daniel," she said carefully, knowing she was treading on very shaky ground, "and the glorious piece of music that came out of it, is life-changing." She paused. "It's already changed mine."

The angry set of his mouth relaxed only slightly. "What are you talking about?"

"I can't help wondering, Dan, about some of the things you wrote in your journal. Why were they true five years ago but not today?" She took a deep breath, then decided that after going this far, she couldn't quit now. "Has God changed in the meantime?"

She was amazed at her own insolence. She prayed she wasn't going beyond the point of forgiveness.

"What exactly are you trying to say?" The anger he was so obviously fighting to keep under control was like a physical blow to Jennifer. Thunder, much closer now, rolled and slammed against the house, a fitting accompaniment to the fury blazing in his eyes. Jennifer shivered involuntarily when lightning crackled and lighted the darkness outside the floor-to-ceiling glass windows.

Suddenly her thoughts went crazy and an enormous wave of guilt washed over her. Who did she think she was, violating his privacy like this? She had come here, intent upon trying to shock him out of his depression. But she'd never intended to hurt him. He had been hurt enough. Certainly she didn't want to be the one to inflict even more.

Her eyes began to sting and she wished she'd never begun any of this. She felt as though she were losing her already tenuous grip on something very fragile, but very, very precious.

"Dan—" She heard the uncertainty in her voice. And so, apparently, had he.

"Don't stop now, Jennifer." His face could have been carved in stone.

She took a deep breath, then spilled the words out in one jumbled rush. "Everything you tried to tell me . . . it was all true."

Still he remained motionless, an impassive statue.

"You were right . . . about all of it."

He gave a small shake of his head and frowned. "What *are* you talking about?"

She squeezed her eyes shut for an instant, then opened them again and studied him through her tears, relieved to see that his anger appeared to be ebbing. Now he simply looked confused.

"Your journal. The things you wrote . . . "

His frown deepened. "What about it?"

"Oh, Daniel . . . it broke my heart! And don't you see? That's exactly what had to happen! I had to be broken—completely broken—before God could put the pieces back together the way He wanted them. You can't mend something that isn't broken!"

Her words spun between them, churning into an echo that bounced across the hollow recesses of the pool house. Hesitantly, she took a step, then another, until she had closed the distance between them. Her heart was in her throat, and the pains shooting upward from her ribcage nearly stopped her movement. She hadn't realized until now how tightly she was holding herself together.

Finally, when she was close enough to touch him, she stopped and stood perfectly still, raising her eyes to study with infinite caring his strong, firmly molded features. A look that was at once forlorn and hopeful now gentled his smoldering expression of moments before.

Unable to help herself, she lifted an unsteady hand and lightly touched her fingertips to his face. "Daniel . . . I understand now. What you've tried for so long to tell me. About having faith enough to trust God's love. About His right to work His will in our lives . . . even when it seems He's being unfair or that He's only doling out punishment and pain." She paused. Perhaps it no longer made any difference to him, but she had to tell him, had to share this life-changing explosion that had occurred in her spirit.

"In your journal . . . when you finally came to Romans 8:28—*"And we know that God causes all things to work together for good to those who love God . . . . "* That's the message of *Daybreak*, too, isn't it? That God took the ugliest, most shameful symbol ever known—the cross—and turned it into glory. That what seemed to be the most awful event in history was changed into the most *important* event in history."

Even in the face of his passivity, Jennifer couldn't control her newfound joy. "Oh, Dan, don't you see? I'm *free* now! I'm not angry anymore. I don't have to fight God anymore! You already knew all this, but I had to find it out for myself! And I did! Because of *you!* It was all there, in your journal, and in *Daybreak*."

For a long moment, it was as though he would never move again, and Jennifer dropped her hand away from his face, let it fall slowly to her side in reluctant defeat.

"Maybe it doesn't matter anymore," she said in a near whisper as she stared upward at his face, her own agony apparent in her voice. "But I just had to tell you." Her final words were nearly lost in the repeated crash of thunder that shook the windows of the house.

Dan's sightless eyes slowly filled with tears, and he tried to turn away from her. But she saw and grasped his shoulders with both hands, holding him. "No—don't turn away from me, Dan. Don't shut me out, please."

Had she caused the grief that washed across his face

when he slowly turned back to her? "Jennifer . . . I can't—" He swallowed with obvious difficulty. "You deserve so much more than I can give you."

"I don't *want* anything more than you can give me! I just want *you*." She looked up at him, her eyes glowing and filled with love and determination. "I want to be your wife, Dan."

"Jennifer, don't you see?" he asked miserably. "I can't look after you the way a man should be able to." His despair was almost a tangible thing. "I couldn't even protect a retarded little boy . . . or my own dog. That could have been *you* that day! You could have taken the bullets meant for me—and I wouldn't even have known you were in danger!"

The words exploded from him, a harsh, agonized cry that stunned Jennifer into momentary silence.

Her eyes widened with the slow dawn of understanding. "Is *that* what's wrong?"

He didn't answer.

"It *is*, isn't it? You're punishing yourself with guilt! Because you tried to bait this lunatic to come after you while I was gone, to protect me. And then Jason and Sunny got hurt—"

He grabbed her arm in an almost painful vise. "Yes! And *I* caused it! It was my stupid pride, my stubbornness again!" Abruptly, as though he realized he might be hurting her, he gentled his grasp on her arm.

"I thought I could handle it," he said harshly. "That's always been my way. To handle things on my own."

His jaw tensed and he shook his head at her small cry of protest. "I thought, after the accident, that I'd finally gotten rid of that insufferable pride of mine. I even reached the point where I could accept help from people without getting all steamed up about it." He gave a nasty, short laugh. "You'd expect me to have a healthy dose of humility after I had to learn to eat and brush my teeth and fry an egg all over again, wouldn't you?"

Tears trickled slowly down Jennifer's cheeks as, outside, the sky finally released its pentup deluge amidst the growling thunder and streaks of lightning.

"Then you came along." His gentle smile of wonder—the first sign of his former tenderness she'd seen in days—nearly broke her heart. "And suddenly I needed my pride back all over again." He reached out a tenuous hand to lightly graze one side of her face. "I wanted to be . . . enough for you. I wanted to be what you thought I was—some kind of spiritual giant."

Jennifer blanched. It was true. That's exactly what she had made of him in her mind.

His smile now turned bitter. "I may have made a half-hearted attempt to convince you I wasn't what you seemed to think, but the truth of the matter was that I enjoyed your fantasy. I wanted to be exactly what you thought I was. Strong. Capable. Independent. It didn't take too long for the old proud spirit to kick into gear again and convince me I could handle a—*normal* relationship with you. Love. Marriage. A family. I wanted it all. I wanted to be . . . as much to you as any other man could be. Knowing all the time it was impossible."

She closed her eyes. When she could finally bring herself to look at him again, her heart wrenched to see the tears that had spilled over from his eyes were now falling freely down his sun-bronzed cheeks.

"Oh, Dan," she murmured with dismay, "haven't you forgotten something?" She didn't wait for him to say anything more. "You say you couldn't protect a retarded little boy or your own dog. But Dan . . . I'm neither. I'm a grown woman. You don't have to watch over me. I can watch over myself. Daniel—I don't need you to *protect* me. I need you to *love* me!"

Somehow she made her way into his arms. She felt the

strong shoulders that had cradled her and comforted her in the past now heave and slump. He leaned against her, burying his face in the cloud of her hair ... and he wept.

Jennifer now fully understood his former pain and his near-ruin, the hopelessness that had very nearly defeated and destroyed him five years before. Her face was soaked with his tears and her own, and she was blind now, too, her vision blurred by their mingled tears. Outside, the night sky wept with them, and the mountain roared as though in its own agony. But Jennifer knew nothing except the man whose hurt she now tried to absorb into her own heart. She held him as tenderly as she would have a child, promising him silently he would never again bear his pain alone.

And she knew then, as she could never have known before, how it must have been for him after the accident. She saw with the clarity of a blue-white flash of lightning that suddenly blazed outside the house how wrong, how incredibly wrong, she had been about the man who now wept in her arms. She saw how weak he must have been, and realized for the first time the infinite amount of strength the Lord had given him, the awesome quality of faith He had woven from that weakness. She saw how very far her beloved had actually come. Such a long, hard way.

"Jennifer ... I need you ... "

She nodded, and murmured softly against his bearded cheek.

" ... You make me whole ... you make me a man again ... "

" ... I love you, Daniel ... "

" ... You really will marry me ... "

" ... Oh, yes, love, of course, I'll marry you ... "

" ... Soon ... "

" ... Whenever you say ... "

The fury roaring outside the house muted the shrill ringing

186

of the phone. "Dan—the phone—"

Ever so slowly, he quieted and, lifting his head, wiped the dampness from his eyes with the back of his arm. "Would you get it?"

Moving reluctantly out of his embrace, Jennifer walked to the wall phone and lifted the receiver.

It was Pauline. As soon as Jennifer answered, Dan's mother exploded with the good news. "Jennifer—Jason is conscious! He's asking for Dan! Lucas just called. Tell Dan that Jason is going to be all right!"

Her excited voice carried across to where Dan was standing, and when Jennifer glanced over at him, she saw him whisper to himself . . . *My dear Lord . . . thank you . . . thank you, Father . . .*

"Yes—I'll drive him to the hospital. We'll go right away!" Jennifer hung up and moved to give Dan a relieved hug. "You *do* want to go, don't you?"

"Just as soon as I get dressed!" He started moving toward the dressing room. "Listen, while I change clothes, why don't you go in and tell Rick he can go, that we're going to be leaving?"

"Oh—my goodness, I'd forgotten that he was even *here!*"

Dan grinned—his old grin, the one Jennifer loved to distraction. "Yeah . . . I know what you mean."

Jennifer poked her head out the door to watch the patrol car pull out of the driveway. The rain was blowing so hard it sprayed her face, even though the porch overhang helped to break the wind. She was halfway back inside the door when something caught her attention.

The headlights of the patrol car flashed across the east side of the house as Rick backed out, momentarily illuminating the dense grove of mature pine trees only yards away. Jennifer stuck her head out even further, ignoring the wind-driven rain blowing in against her. She had seen something . . . something red, she was sure of it, out there amidst the trees. Craning her neck as far as possible to avoid stepping out onto the porch, she squinted into the darkness. But the lights from the patrol car were gone now, and she could see nothing but rain swept shadows.

Still, she waited uneasily, thinking a flash of lightning might give enough light for her to catch another glimpse of whatever she'd seen. She didn't have to wait long. An eerie blue-white glow suddenly framed the entire lot, followed by the insistent banging of a series of thunderclaps. Jennifer winced, drawing her shoulders forward and involuntarily squeezing her eyes shut, missing the split-second opportunity to get another look at the tree-shrouded field.

"Dummy," she accused herself irritably as she bounced back inside and shut the door hard behind her.

She stood there for a moment, her back against the door, trying to shake off her nearly irrational fear of the storm. She'd been this way ever since she was a toddler without ever knowing why. After a few shaky gulps of air, she turned and started to walk back through the dining area and kitchen to return to Dan in the pool house.

She had just begun to feel a slight ebbing of her panic when a dazzling bolt of lightning seemed to ram straight into the ground outside the window at her right. Wide-eyed, Jennifer stopped dead, riveted by the iridescent explosion, then screamed at the following boom of thunder that shook the mountain and plunged the house into total darkness.

18

Jennifer's blood froze from her head to her feet. For a long, breathless moment, she could do nothing but stand motionless, almost paralyzed with shock.

The darkness around her was as thick as ink. She felt lightheaded and wondered fleetingly if she were about to faint. No, she couldn't. She had to get to Dan. She had to tell him about the lights. *But it wouldn't matter to Dan that the lights were out . . . it would only matter to her.*

She pushed a white-knuckled fist against her mouth to keep from screaming again, then dropped it to her side, clenching her hands tightly together in front of her. After two or three ragged breaths, she began to move toward the open door of the pool house.

She stumbled around the kitchen counter, hit the side of the refrigerator, then kicked Sunny's food dish on the floor.

Finally she was able to grab the doorframe. She stopped just inside the entrance, peering down the length of the pool.

"Dan?" She squinted into the warm dampness of the room. "Dan, the power's out. Should I call—"

Her question died on her lips when she halted in mid-step and gasped in stunned horror. Lightning was flashing regularly every few seconds, shedding enough light through the floor-to-ceiling windows to reveal two shadows close to the door of the dressing room. On the other wall, the outside door stood open, an ominous, gaping black hole. Jennifer realized that one of the shadows—the larger one—was Dan. He appeared to be facing the wall, while the other shadow pushed something against him.

She was too disoriented by the storm and the sudden darkness to assimilate the indistinct scene taking place in front of her eyes. It was only when a rolling ball of lightning streaked across the outside, illuminating the pool house in the aftermath of its glow, that she realized Dan was pinned against the wall by a man holding a gun in his back!

Too terrified to be cautious, she screamed. The gun-wielding man whirled toward her, his corpse-like face illuminated for a dazzling instant, framed for all time in her memory. It was the same cadaverous face she had seen peering in her kitchen window!

She lunged forward, intent only upon helping Dan, but when the man waved the gun and took a wild shot at her, she fell crashing to the floor. She lay there, watching in dazed terror as she saw Dan pivot around and snake his foot out in a low, unbelievably accurate kick that knocked his assailant off-balance and sent him sprawling, arms waving, into the pool. The gun sailed out of his hand and went bouncing over the tiled floor, echoing loudly all the way down the room.

Jennifer hauled herself awkwardly to her knees, but stopped dead when Dan yelled at her. "*Jennifer—get the gun!*"

She stared at him blankly for an instant, then glanced over the floor, trying to find the gun. There it was, lying only inches from the rim of the pool. Looking back to Dan, she saw that he had shrugged out of his robe and was now smoothly sliding off the side of the pool into the water after the man who had just fallen in.

Her mind stuck on a blank screen, numbed by the whirlwind of events, frozen to inaction by her fear. She could feel a tight thread of hysteria threatening to snap somewhere deep inside her. Her brain began to spin out of control, and she was able to hold onto her reason only by sheer force of will—and the awareness that Dan was alone in the pool with a madman.

"Daniel, what are you doing? I'll come in with you. You can't see where he—"

"*No!*" he called back over his shoulder. "I can't keep track of you *and* him! Just stay quiet so I can hear—and *get the gun!*"

Still she hesitated, taking a couple of steps closer to the side of the pool, then stepping back again to watch Dan as he went under. She knew she had to move, she had to get the gun. *But shouldn't I go in and help him . . . he can't see, . . . how will he be able to find him? No, Dan said not to come in. And he's right, it might make it worse . . . then he'd be trying to take care of me, too . . . Oh, dear Lord, please don't let Dan be hurt!*

Her stomach clenched with revulsion as she forced herself to pick up the gun. She held it extended outward from her body as far as possible, staring at it as though it were something alive and extremely deadly.

Dan felt the water enfold him like a soft, smooth blanket as he pushed himself easily away from the side and began to quietly bob up and down, listening and waiting. Within seconds he had a fix on direction and also knew for certain his assailant was panicking in the water. But there was no time to waste; the man could regain his senses any moment.

He went under the water with one smooth scissors motion and began to push forward slowly but confidently. The pressure in his ears and on his lungs was nothing in comparison to the enormity of desperation he felt. He *had* to find him—he had to take him. To get him away from Jennifer. Who *was* this guy, anyway? Someone he knew? What had he done to cause this kind of irrational hatred in the man?

The muffled exclamations above the surface of the water

were much louder now. He began to feel the current lapping against his face from the thrashing motions the man was making with his legs. He was getting close. Very close.

Dan knew he had all the advantages for a few more seconds. The sensation was rare, but exhilarating. He had lived too long with the handicapped person's continual awareness of always being at a disadvantage not to appreciate the feeling of being on top for a change. He had another plus in that he was still in his swimming trunks, while the other man, he was sure, was fully clothed. The weight of that soggy clothing would badly inhibit his movement in the water, even pull him under.

Best of all, the lights were out. His assailant would be as much in the dark as he himself was. In addition, Dan had caught a strong scent of liquor when the man had first broken through the door and pinned him against the wall. The few rough words he'd heard had been slurred and incoherent.

As he swam silently and determinedly, he felt a change in the ripples only a few yards away and knew that the man had begun to move in spite of his panic. The indistinct yelling sounded farther away, and the current from the churning of the water also began to move away from Dan. He followed the movement and the sound as closely as he dared, staying under the water and remaining totally quiet.

Until he knew he had him.

He soared up through the water in one swooping motion, his hand extended palm outward to feel for the man's face so he could be certain of taking him from behind. As soon as he felt the back of the man's head, Dan raised both powerful arms directly above him and began to push him straight down into the water. The man waved his arms wildly, cursing and screaming, then striking Dan in the face several times before catching him in the midriff with his elbow. But Dan was much bigger and in far better condition. Every move the smaller man made was in vain. Finally, with one large, powerful hand, Dan pushed him under the water and followed him down.

The man tried to fight, but was quickly pulled to the pool bottom by the weight of his clothes and his own panic. Dan refused to let go of him. He followed him to the bottom and efficiently locked an iron forearm around his neck from behind in a relentless hold.

Jennifer stood by the side of the pool, staring wide-eyed with terror into the darkness of the water, seeing the dark blobs of movement beneath the surface. With one trembling, clammy hand she gripped the gun in a death vise, steadying it with her other hand.

They had been below for what seemed like hours. She waited, barely breathing, knowing all the while she should run to the phone and call the police, yet unable to move until she knew whether Dan was all right. She knew what he'd said, but if they didn't come up in the next few seconds, she was going in. She even pulled her tennis shoes off in preparation. How much longer should she wait? How long could they stay down? If they didn't come up soon . . . .

She screamed and nearly dropped the gun when a wave of water sprayed her in the face as both men suddenly broke above the surface. Weak with relief, she saw Dan swim to the side of the pool, dragging the other man along with him. When he reached the pool wall, he hauled himself partly up out of the water, holding his assailant securely with one arm until he could pull the unconscious man up behind him.

"Jennifer—"

She was already beside him. "Dan! Are you all right? Is he—"

Jennifer paused, momentarily stunned by the flare of light as the electricity suddenly returned. "Dan!" she exclaimed.

"The lights! The lights are back on!"

Dan was panting heavily with exertion, but he waved a hand to calm her down. "Good! Take a look at this guy. Who is he anyway? Do you recognize him?"

Jennifer, still shaking, replied, "I don't know his name, but he's the man at my house the other night."

Dan nodded as if he weren't surprised. Flipping the still unconscious man over on his back, he knelt beside him and lowered his head to listen to his chest. "He swallowed most of the pool. I'm going to have to pump him out."

He raised the man's head and checked his airway, then flipped him, none too gently, Jennifer noticed, onto his stomach and began applying firm pressure to pump the water from his lungs.

"Jennifer, you better call the police."

She quickly placed the gun on the table and then ran to the pool side phone to dial the police station. Once she'd delivered her message, practically screaming into the receiver, she hurried back to Dan, going to her knees to see if she could help. But Dan already had the man gulping and coughing up water.

"Check his pockets, Jennifer. I'd kinda like to know who we've got here, since he's so bent out of shape about me." He continued to knead the man's back.

Jennifer pulled a soaked, ruined billfold out of the back pocket of the man's khaki work pants and opened it. Everything inside was wet and clinging to the wallet. Her hands were trembling so violently she could hardly function, but she finally managed to separate a driver's license from a credit card. "Okay," she muttered, "here's his license. Let's see—" Jennifer stared down at the wet, laminated card and made a strangled sound of disbelief.

Dan heard her and slowed the movement of his hands on the prostrate form at his side. "What'd you find?"

"*Daniel*—" She was finally able to breathe. "It's—*Caleb Arbegunst!* Jim's father!"

Dan froze in mid-motion. Beneath his hands, the man spewed out water and coughed convulsively. "*Caleb?* Are you sure?"

"That's what it says!" Jennifer continued to stare down at the card in her hands for a moment, then scanned the other papers in the wallet. "Yes—here's a credit card. And . . . here's some kind of social services i.d. They all say the same thing. But *why*, Dan? What does Caleb Arbegunst have against *you?*"

He shook his head as if he were dazed. "I hardly even know the man! I'd only seen him once before the accident, and I've never talked to him since."

Jennifer had nearly forgotten that Caleb Arbegunst had been with the teenage boy who hit Dan's car and caused his blindness. Still, why would he be trying to kill Dan? What possible reason could he have?

"This doesn't make any sense," Dan said in a low, puzzled voice as he rolled the man's body over. "Caleb Arbegunst is almost a stranger to me. I—"

Suddenly he stopped, and Jennifer watched in horror as his face contorted into a chilling rictus of shock. "Dan! What is it? What's wrong?"

He seemed riveted in place, his face frozen in a look of anguish. When he started to shiver, she was afraid he might be going into shock.

Seeing the robe he had tossed by the side of the pool before plunging in after Caleb, she got quickly to her feet and went after it. She returned and draped it gently around Dan's shoulders, letting her hands linger on him until she felt the tremor racking his body slowly begin to subside.

She knelt down beside him and watched him closely. Finally the tension in his face began to relax. He shook his head slowly back and forth as if he were trying to clear his mind. "Something—about the dream, the one I keep having—" He stopped. His shoulders slumped, and he frowned as he grazed the fingers of one hand over the scar at his eyebrow. "I don't know . . . " His voice drifted off.

Both of them jumped in surprise when the man between them strained to raise his upper body off the floor and then began to scream and flail his arms. His bloodshot eyes were wild and disoriented. He looked like a wounded, savage animal. His soaked clothing was plastered to his emaciated body and wet wisps of hair were glued to his skull-shaped head.

Dan moved quickly to pin him to the floor and hold him there. Caleb thrashed and hurled his head from side to side, trying to free himself from Dan's vise-like hold, all the while cursing at them and spewing a barrage of words that made no sense.

Jennifer watched the two of them anxiously. Dan had Caleb locked in a relentless grip, but he looked too shaky to hold on much longer. When she saw him begin to tremble again, she lay her hand uncertainly on his forearm, wishing she knew what to do. He didn't seem to be hurt, but he was obviously in the grip of some kind of emotional upheaval, and he was frightening her.

Suddenly the insane babbling from the man on the floor penetrated her consciousness and she stared down at him in surprise. At the same time, Dan choked off an exclamation and frowned as he tried to listen more closely.

" . . . should have killed you the first time . . . knew it. Knew you'd cause trouble . . . "

"Dan—what is he—"

Dan threw up a hand to silence her. "What trouble, Caleb? What kind of trouble?" He attempted to prompt the crazed, wild-eyed man who continued to ramble in an irrational monotone.

" . . . just waitin' on me, weren't you . . . just bidin' your time to do me in, so you could take my kid . . . thought you'd drive me nuts, didn't you, then you could have my boy with no problem . . . . "

Jennifer felt as if someone were striking her lungs with an enormous hammer, knocking the breath from her. She glanced at Dan and saw the knotted muscles and cords in his arms tighten even more as he lowered his face toward the man he was holding on the floor.

"Dan—what is he talking about?"

Dan shook his head almost violently. "Waiting on what, Caleb?" he said slowly through clenched teeth. "What was I waiting on?"

" . . . all these years, you knew . . . just waitin' to tell, tryin' to make me sick, tryin' to take my boy . . . well, you ain't gonna get him . . . I'll shut you up for good this time, Kaine . . . . "

When he would have reared up like a wild thing, Dan pressed him that much harder to the floor. "Tell what, Caleb? What is it you want to stop me from telling?"

Jennifer framed her face with both hands in sick horror and bewilderment. She looked from Dan, whose face was a mask of self-control, down to Caleb, shaking and thrashing in weak futility.

" . . . you saw me . . . you knew I was drivin' that night . . . they said you couldn't remember anything, but I knew better . . . your memory came back a long time ago, you were just waitin' to tell . . . you waited so you could make me sick and get my boy, didn't you . . . you went and gave him that job, coddled him, took him places, let him swim in your big, fancy pool . . . . "

"Driving?" Daniel echoed hoarsely. "*You* were driving . . . the night of the accident? Not the boy?"

Caleb uttered an ugly snort, and Jennifer felt suddenly nauseated from the stench of alcohol.

197

" . . . I wouldn't let one of those no-good punks drive my truck. He wanted to . . . he said I was drunk . . . I wasn't drunk, never been drunk on the road . . . I'd had a few beers waiting for him, that was all . . . wasn't drunk . . . . "

Jennifer heard no more, the random flow of his words lost to her now as she reached out to grasp Dan's arm, dazed and sickened by what she'd just heard. The man was admitting what he thought Dan already knew. But Jennifer took one look at Dan's face and realized how totally wrong Caleb Arbegunst was. Dan didn't know. He had *never* known!

"Dan . . . is he saying what I think he is?"

Her question fell flatly between them, dying quickly in the silence. Even the storm outside was subsiding. Nothing was left of it except a few weak spurts of lightning and the sound of muffled thunder moving off into the distance. The earlier torrents of rain that had assaulted the house turned to a gentle, rhythmic patter, almost hypnotic in its steady thrum against the metal roof.

Jennifer continued to watch Dan, fearful of what he might do. His grasp on Caleb never faltered or weakened. He was like a kneeling statue, frozen in place, unmoving and unfeeling. The unsteady rhythm of his breathing, the thin line of perspiration that had begun to drape itself along the ridge above his dark brows, the sudden, uncharacteristic paleness that settled over his face were the only hints she could detect of the storm she felt certain must be gathering in his soul.

"You were driving the truck, Caleb?" His voice was ominously quiet. "Not the boy?"

Jennifer had never had such an urge to lash out and strike a man as she did when she heard the high-pitched giggle that came from Caleb's mouth.

" . . . dumb kid, tried to grab the wheel from me . . . coulda got us both killed . . . . "

Dan's face contorted into a thunderous mask of rage. He

moved his hands from Caleb's shoulders, closer to his neck, and Jennifer gasped when she saw his fingers clench and unclench. "Dan—"

"The boy *was* killed, you drunken—" Suddenly he stopped, shook himself almost violently, and Jennifer saw his hands tighten once, then twice, before he moved them back to Caleb's shoulders, holding him just firmly enough to keep him from breaking free.

"You put him under the wheel—after the crash." He made it a statement, not a question.

" . . . yeah . . . you were out cold . . . you didn't see me, nobody saw me . . . he was just a scrawny kid, I pushed him right under the wheel . . . nobody ever knew. They didn't even check me out . . . nobody saw . . . nobody knew . . . . " His red-rimmed, watery eyes cleared and focused for just an instant. "Except you."

Jennifer watched Dan, still afraid he might explode, unable to blame him if he did. The look on his face was peculiar, unreadable, when he answered quietly, "No, Caleb. I never knew. No one knew but you. Until now."

Slowly, little by little, the man on the floor quieted, the insanity temporarily stilled. He stared up at the big man holding him down, unable to grasp or accept the truth of what he was hearing.

" . . . you're lyin' . . . you knew, you always knew . . . you wanted to make me sick . . . you wanted my boy . . . . "

Dan shook his head in a sad, hopeless gesture. "You poor fool," he murmured softly. "You sold out your whole life— even your own son—for a bottle of temporary escape and a soul full of guilt."

Still holding Caleb to the floor, Dan looked like a man coming out from under a long sleep.

"No, Caleb. All I knew was a flash of something in a nightmare. That's all I ever knew—just a bad dream that never seemed to end. Your secret would probably have been safe for a lifetime."

Caleb twisted his head back and forth in violent denial. "No, you knew . . . you always knew . . . you even said on the radio you knew who I was . . . ."

Dan didn't answer right away. When he did, his tone held a note of surprise. "I wasn't talking about the accident. I was just trying to bait you, get you out in the open so you'd make a move. And then I nearly caused Jason and Sunny to get killed. No, man," he said once more, very softly, "I never knew. You were the only one who knew the truth, Caleb."

They heard the sirens then, wailing up the mountain. Jennifer drew the first long breath she'd had in what seemed like hours, and rose trembling to her feet to unlock the door for the police.

But Gabe was already through the door, using the key he always carried. He blasted through the entrance to the pool house, nearly knocking Jennifer to the floor in his panicky resolve to get to Dan. "What happened—what's going on? The police chased me all the way up here!"

Jennifer saw with relief that there was a ghost of a smile on Dan's face when he answered. "Relax, buddy—everything's under control."

Two police officers brandishing drawn revolvers charged in behind Gabe. Dan turned Caleb over to them with noticeable relief and hauled himself wearily to his feet, slipping his arms into the sleeves of his robe as he stood.

Gabe shot questions at his friend like bullets out of a gun, and Dan gave him a few brief but concise answers, then held up a restraining hand. "Do me a favor—please. Take everyone into the house. Give me a minute."

Jennifer thought he sounded extremely tired. Gabe darted a questioning look at her, and she tried to give him a weak, reassuring smile.

Dan dragged in a long, patient breath, then continued. "I need to be alone . . . just for a few minutes, okay?" He paused only an instant, then added, "Then, if someone will take me, I want to go to the hospital and see my boy."

"Isn't anyone going to tell me what's happened up here?" Gabe's voice was testy and sharp.

"Jennifer," Dan said calmly, "talk to the man, would you? I'm going to get into some dry clothes."

Jennifer stood with Gabe and watched Dan as he turned and began walking slowly down the side of the pool toward the dressing room. She thought with admiration that Dan was the only man she'd ever known who could wear a terry cloth beach wrap with as much style as a royal robe.

He kept on walking, her stricken prince, and she saw his slumped shoulders gradually lift and finally straighten in the familiar mantle of determined strength he wore so easily and so well.

He stopped abruptly beside the aluminum poolside table and after a slight hesitation whipped the cane he'd left lying there into his hand. For a moment he stood unmoving, as if he were making a decision. Then, with a jaunty flick of his wrist, he tossed the cane lightly up into the air, caught it easily on its descent, and sent it sailing smoothly into the deepest part of the pool.

Jennifer couldn't see his face, only his back . . . but she knew he was wearing that vagabond grin of his.

Epilogue

Daniel felt the warmth and the beauty and the special hush of hope in the sanctuary that was unique to Easter Sunday as the choir stirred slightly, readying themselves for the finale of *Daybreak*.

He heard Jennifer's voice begin the solo that would build and then build again before the ending. He had once wondered whether he would ever find it possible to separate that glorious, praising voice of hers from the low, endearing voice of the woman he loved.

But just as it had during rehearsals, her voice began to move him to worship. As it did, he realized anew that one of the miracles of her gift, one of the wonders of her voice, was that the Lord seemed to raise it, temporarily, above human things, using it to bring hearts to their knees in simple worship. For the next few moments, she would no longer be his Jennifer, his beloved, but instead, she would be an instrument of praise.

With that thought, he straightened his shoulders and readied himself for what he knew he and the entire congregation were about to experience. He smiled to himself in anticipation and silently thanked his Lord for all the doors He had closed and all the channels He had opened to lead Jennifer to this place . . . to him, to the music, and to her new peace of spirit.

He gave thanks, as he so often had, that her voice, deemed less than enough for the operatic stage, was so wonderfully perfect for the Lord's use. And then he simply listened and let his own spirit soar along with the voice and the music . . . .

Slowly, Jennifer returned from the place the music had taken her. She opened her eyes and saw Dan standing there, smiling to himself, yet smiling at her, too, and she knew once more that, even though he couldn't see her face, he was seeing her heart. He was looking deep inside her, seeing what was there and loving what he saw.

As she held the last note and heard it echo and fade into the silent sanctuary, she thanked her Lord for the light He had poured into her heart, into her spirit . . . and into their love, hers and Daniel's.

She smiled a little when the choir breathed a collective sigh with the congregation. Lyss, standing next to her, squeezed her hand; Gabe, at the end of the same row, gave her an uncommonly serious nod of affirmation.

She watched the effect of the music gradually lift away from the congregation, seeing many of them dry their eyes before flinging themselves to their feet in a combined accolade to the Lord, to the choir and to Daniel.

She saw the proud, happy faces of her dad and Loren smiling up at her. And she watched little Jason—her future son—grin from ear to ear as he waved uninhibitedly to her. She smiled at Jim, sitting between Dan's parents who now had temporary custody of the boy, thinking it was the first time she had ever seen him looking happy and healthy and unafraid.

Her eyes filled when she saw Dan finally relax his shoulders from this monumental effort into which he had poured so much of his heart and soul. He wiped a handkerchief across his forehead and dabbed at his cheeks. Then he turned around to the congregation and raised one hand in a sweeping motion of tribute to the choir and the large wooden cross that stood behind them. Finally, he turned back to the choir and gently smiled in Jennifer's direction . . . and her spirit started to sing all over again.

As the choir began to leave the platform, she waited for him. Together the two of them, along with Sunny, walked down the aisle, following the choir out while the congregation waited. When they were almost to the door, Dan took her hand and placed it snugly on his forearm, covering it with his own.

"Is the sun shining this morning, love?"

Jennifer glanced up at his smiling face, then down at her hand and the diamond solitaire gleaming there. The ring captured a sunbeam, a rainbow of light streaking in through the stained glass window nearby.

"Oh, yes, Daniel," she answered, glancing from her ring up to his face. "The sun is definitely shining this morning."